COLLECTION TWO

Juliet nearly a Vet

4 BOOKS IN ONE

REBECCA JOHNSON

Illustrated by Kyla May

Puffin Books

PUFFIN BOOKS

UK | USA | Canada | Ireland | Australia
India | New Zealand | South Africa | China

Penguin Books is part of the Penguin Random House group of companies
whose addresses can be found at global.penguinrandomhouse.com.

Penguin
Random House
Australia

First published by Penguin Random House Australia Pty Ltd, 2014
This collection published by Penguin Random House Australia Pty Ltd, 2017

13 5 7 9 10 8 6 4 2

Cover and text design of individual stories by
Karen Scott © Penguin Random House Australia Pty Ltd
Collection cover design by Tony Palmer © Penguin Random House Australia Pty Ltd
Author photograph by Megan Peacock
Typeset in New Century Schoolbook
Colour separation by Splitting Image Colour Studio, Clayton, Victoria
Printed and bound in Australia by Griffin Press, an accredited ISO AS/NZS 14001
Environmental Management Systems printer

National Library of Australia Cataloguing-in-Publication data:

Johnson, Rebecca
Juliet, nearly a vet collection 2/ Rebecca Johnson; illustrated by Kyla May.

ISBN: 978 0 14 378692 4

penguin.com.au

Hi! I'm Juliet. I'm ten years old.
And I'm nearly a vet!

I bet you're wondering how someone who is only ten
could nearly be a vet. It's pretty simple really.
My mum's a vet. I watch what she does and
I help out all the time. There's really not that
much to it, you know...

Juliet
nearly a
Vet

Beach Buddies

CHAPTER
1

Vets never stop being vets

'*Come on*, Juliet, or we'll be setting up the tent in the dark!'

I can hear that Dad's starting to lose his cool.

'Coming,' I call as I try to stuff a couple more things into my vet kit that used to be Dad's fishing box. I manage to snap one clip closed but the other just won't budge.

I stagger out the front door with my load, and the look of horror on Dad's face says it all. The car is packed to the roof in the back and there's not much room left.

'No way! You are not bringing all that with you,' says Dad, shaking his head.

My best friend Chelsea is on her way over from her house next door. She's coming camping with us and we're so excited. She's got a neat little backpack that takes up about a quarter of the space mine does, but most of my gear is vet equipment. You never know what emergencies might come up on a trip, so I have to be prepared for anything.

'Don't worry, Dad,' I say soothingly. 'It can all go under our feet. I like having my feet up in the car.'

'And where's the dog going to sit?'

'On my lap, of course!'

'Juliet, it's a four-hour trip. The dog is not going to just lie on your lap happily the whole time.'

'He can sit on mine, too,' Chelsea pipes up helpfully.

'And mine,' says Max, trying to open a lollipop and hold three dinosaurs at once.

'Fine, suit yourselves. But I don't want to hear any whingeing.'

'Who's whingeing?' says Mum as she pulls the front door closed.

'No one, yet . . .' grumbles Dad.

We haven't even made it out of

our street before poor Curly breaks wind. It must be the excitement of coming on holidays with us. I look over at Chelsea and I can see her eyes starting to water as she desperately tries to breathe through her shirt.

Max howls with laughter. I'll never really understand the way boys think.

We start playing I-spy and the alphabet game, but we're sick of that after twenty minutes.

'Did you bring your grooming kit, Chelsea?'

'Of course,' says Chelsea, patting the bag at her feet. 'Although I'm not sure there will be many animals to groom at the beach.'

'I guess you can always practise on Curly.'

Max has fallen asleep sucking a lollipop. His mouth is hanging open and the lollipop is in danger of falling out, so I place one of his dinosaurs under his chin to prop it shut. Curly is panting in my face and wagging his tail in Chelsea's, so it's getting pretty squashy. Every now and then Dad looks into the back at us and we try our best to look like we are having a very comfortable time. I can see he's just waiting for us to whinge, but it's not going to happen.

'Did you bring your vet kit, Mum?' I say.

'No, honey, I didn't. I'm on holidays and there will be vet surgeries nearby if an animal's in trouble.'

I look at Chelsea and we both shake our heads and I roll my eyes. Mum should know better. A vet never knows when an emergency is going to happen.

Curly eventually lies down and goes to sleep and I'm able to reach my Vet Diary from my bag. Chelsea and I start to make a list of the animals we might see on a beach camping holiday.

Seagulls
Fish
Pelicans
Crabs
Dolphins

When we finally drive into the
campground it's well after lunch. It's
taken us longer because Max threw
up (Mum thinks he overdid it on the
lollies) and Dad kept stopping to let
Curly out to see if he needed to go to
the toilet after a few too many really
bad smells.

I can see Chelsea is nearly weeping
tears of joy when Mum says we're
here.

'Don't go wandering off too far, or
near the water,' says Mum. 'We'll need
you to help us carry all the stuff into
the tent once we get it set up.'

The best thing is Curly gets to sleep
in the tent with us. Our tent is really

big and has two separate rooms. Chelsea,
Max, Curly and I have one room, and
Mum and Dad are in the other.

We race off to explore. The camping
ground is amazing. We've only just
arrived and I could already fill a whole

page with the animals we've seen.
I can't wait to explore the rock pools
and beach this afternoon. Vets need
to know about all kinds of animals
because vets are vets, even when they
are on holidays.

CHAPTER 2

Vets need to be kind to all animals

We set our beds up in the tent. Chelsea's going to sleep on the air bed in the middle between Max and me. She spends ages making her bed really neat and even has a little cushion and some soft toys. Max hasn't got his sleeping bag out yet, but he has arranged his dinosaurs all around the edges of the tent.

'They're going to get in the way, Max,' I say, swiping a few aside.

'Hey!' whines Max. 'Don't hit them!'
He crawls straight over Chelsea's neat
bed to pick them up.

'Why did you have to bring so many
dinosaurs anyway?' I grumble.

I make room for my vet kit, my
emergency rescue pack (this has some
extra things for special situations that
I wouldn't normally carry in my vet
kit, like Grandad's old binoculars), and
my pet carrier, which I also brought in
case of an emergency.

When we're all set up and Chelsea has
re-made her bed, it's time to go to the
beach. We take off, running down the
track and leaping over the dunes onto

the soft, white sand below.

It's late afternoon and there's hardly anyone on the beach, but I can see a couple of fishermen standing out in the surf. Curly is going crazy running up and down the beach, grabbing sticks and bringing them back. Dad throws them way down the beach and Curly charges off after

them. Mum and Dad start walking and we follow along behind, but we keep stopping to look at all the interesting stuff that's washed up.

'Hey, check this out,' yells Max. He's found a large piece of coral that is bleached white from the sun.

We're almost in line with the fishermen now and I can see that they

have a bucket sitting up higher on the sand. Chelsea and I have a look to see if there's anything in it. There are some long red worms. They must be going to use them for bait.

'I think they are beachworms, Chelsea. I read about them once. The fishermen drag a rotten fish over the sand to catch them. The worms pop up and they grab them for bait.'

I feel a bit sorry for the worms as they slide around in the bottom of the bucket.

Chelsea looks sad and turns away from them.

'Oh no,' she says. 'Look at this!'

A small tidal creek is flowing back

into the ocean and some little fish are trapped. They are flipping about in what is quickly becoming less and less water.

'We've got to save them!' I gasp, looking around for something to put them in. There are far too many to carry in our hands and we would drop them on the sand.

I see the fishermen's bucket and wonder if they would mind us using it. It's an emergency, after all!

I run down to the water's edge and try to call out to them. The wind throws the noise of the waves and my calls back into my face and the fishermen don't turn around.

Chelsea looks really worried when I run back up to her. I can see she's getting upset.

'Juliet, I think they'll die if we don't get them to the water very soon.'

'We'll have to take the bucket and get some water,' I say, grabbing it and racing down to the surf. Mum and Dad and Max are way up the beach now, and we don't have time to get them.

We get to the water's edge, and I gently tip the bucket to the side to let some more water in. The bucket is now a quarter full and already the worms look a lot happier.

'Just a bit more,' I say, tilting the bucket forward just as a huge wave hits. The bucket is bowled over with us and I look up just in time to see the worms happily heading off in every direction.

'Whoops!' We look out at the fishermen who still have their backs to us.

'Perhaps if we put the bucket back when we're finished they won't even notice?' giggles Chelsea, and we grab it and race up the beach.

We quickly scoop each and every little fish into the bucket of water. They dart around looking for a way to escape.

'It's okay,' I say soothingly. 'We're going to save you.'

We lug the bucket to the sea then slowly tip it. The tiny fish leap into the ocean.

'There,' says Chelsea. 'Already it was worth coming camping.'

We put the bucket back where it

was and charge up the beach to tell
Mum. We leave out the bit about the
worms.

Curly runs up and tries to pass
Dad his most recent treasure – a dead
mullet.

'Oh that is gross!' laughs Max.

The fish has been dead for a while
and is stiff from the sun, but Curly
is overjoyed by his find. He keeps
pushing it into Dad's leg to get him
to throw it.

'Yuck, no, Curly!' Dad yells as the
dog chases him around on the sand.
Dad grabs the fish by the tail and
hurls it into the ocean. Curly starts
to whine and looks out to sea, but his

treasure is lost in the waves. Curly
looks very sad.

Dad is now rubbing his hands in
the sand, trying to get the smell off his
fingers. He keeps sniffing them and
pulling faces that make Max laugh
even more.

We turn around and head back for
camp. I can't wait to light the fire
and start toasting our marshmallows.
Up ahead we can see the fishermen
coming out of the surf and heading
towards their bucket.

Chelsea and I look at each other.

'Wow! Look at this shell, Mum!' I say.

'And this one, Mr Fletcher,' says
Chelsea.

We keep Mum and Dad occupied
for a while and glance up at the men.
One is peering into the bucket and
the other is scratching his head and
looking around on the sand. After a
while they pick up the bucket and
head off.

'We can look for more shells
tomorrow,' says Mum. 'It's time to go
up for a shower now.'

Chelsea and I race ahead.

On the way, Chelsea and I hear
something that sounds really big in
the long grass beside the path.

'What's that?' said Chelsea,
grabbing my arm.

I try to sound very scientific and

brave, but the noise does sound like something big.

'It's probably just a feral cat or something. I've got a page about them in my Vet Diary,' I say, and we both sprint for the safety of the camping ground.

CHAPTER 3

Vets can't be afraid of the dark

'Honey, what happened to those leftover sausages that were beside the barbecue?' Dad looks at Curly suspiciously. Curly wags his tail. Dad shakes his head.

'That's odd,' says Mum. 'Curly has been sitting here with me the whole time. You'd think we would have seen him. Perhaps it was a kookaburra?'

We all look up into the trees as the sun begins to set. Dad is not convinced.

'Can we light the fire now?' I ask.

❖

'Toasted marshmallows are the
yummiest things I've ever eaten,' says
Max, licking sticky goo off his fingers as
we all sit around the fire a little while
later. The warmth on our faces and the
way the flames flick up into the air
makes me feel all cosy and happy.

'That might do you for tonight, Max,' says Mum, as he reaches for another marshmallow, 'or you might be sick again.'

We go and clean our teeth then crawl into our sleeping bags. I'm exhausted and fall straight to sleep, but not for long.

As soon as Mum and Dad lie down, Curly starts to bark. He isn't used to the sounds of the bush. Dad snaps at him to be quiet, but he doesn't stop.

Dad unzips our side of the tent and comes in. *'Oww!'* he yelps, as he steps on one of Max's dinosaurs.

'I told him not to put them there,' I say, 'but he never listens.' I shine the torch on Max. He's asleep with a dinosaur sitting on his chest.

We finally get Curly to settle down, and I drift back into a deep sleep.

❖

'Juliet, wake up!' Chelsea has the torch shining in my face and she's shaking my shoulder. 'Wake up. I can hear something and so can Curly.'

I rub my eyes and try to focus.

'What?'

'I can hear something outside the tent. There's something moving around out there.'

I look over at Curly. His ears are pricked up and he's growling in a low, deep rumble. I pat him and try to calm him down so he doesn't start barking again.

The reflection of the torch on the sides of the tent makes Chelsea's eyes look huge and very worried.

'It's fine, Chelsea. I'll go and have a look.'

'No!' she yelps, grabbing my arm. 'I've been thinking about this. We heard something big in the grass today, now some meat has gone missing so . . . there is something big out there that eats meat! Juliet . . . it might eat you!'

Chelsea's lip starts to quiver and she looks a bit teary. I consider waking my mum, but vets have to be brave sometimes, so I decide to unzip the tent just a tiny bit to see if I can see anything.

Curly, as usual, is very enthusiastic. He tries to shove his nose through the small space and starts sniffing like mad. It takes all my strength to pull his head back out of the hole. 'Can you hold onto him, Chelsea? The last thing we need is him waking Dad up.'

I lie down on my stomach and peer out through the gap. I can't see anything at first, but then a movement catches my eye. There *is* something out there!

'Can you see it?' Chelsea's croaky whisper makes me jump. Curly licks my ear. I hold up my hand in a stop sign and take another minute to look. I grab the torch and shine it in the direction of the movement, and then I see it!

I turn to Chelsea and put my finger to my lips, then I slowly unzip the tent and start to crawl out quietly. Curly squeezes out beside me. Chelsea is still holding onto his collar. Dogs are not very patient at times. I must write that in my Vet Diary later.

We finally all manage to squeeze out of the tent and I shine the torch up into the tree beside our camp site. There, huddled on a branch and peering down at us, is a ring-tailed

possum with a gorgeous joey next to
her. The three of us sit quietly and
watch them watching us. Curly's used
to possums, because we raised some
babies in our home after a big bushfire.

I sweep the beam of light around
the other branches, looking to see what
other nocturnal animals are around.

'Look at that!' Chelsea points to a branch up higher. There is a large owl sitting on it and staring down at us.

'That's a barn owl!' I say.

'How do you know?'

'I can tell from its heart-shaped face and the creamy underparts, and those black spots on its wings. They're common all over Australia and eat small rats and mice. That's why they like campgrounds. People leave food around, so rats and mice come.'

'You really are nearly a vet, aren't you?' sighs Chelsea. 'But can we go back to bed now . . . before the rats and mice turn up?'

CHAPTER
4

Vets need to teach others

We're all a bit tired the next morning.
There were so many different sounds
outside our tent last night that poor
Curly just couldn't relax and spent
most of the night barking to protect
us. Dad says Curly's the one that's
going to need protection if he barks
like that again.

But nothing can spoil our mood
as we head to the beach for a swim
after breakfast, then on to explore the
rock pools. They are crystal clear and

32

filled with life. Each one is like a little
garden underwater. We see starfish,
crabs and colourful little fish darting
from one rock to another. If you sit
really still without your shadow over
a rock pool, after a while, all the
creatures come out from their hiding
spots. Chelsea and I sit for ages near

one with Mum and she helps us add
more creatures to our list.

ROCK POOL CREATURES:

Fish
Crabs
Sea anemones
Starfish
Oysters
Coral (and I thought it was a plant!)
Sponges
Flat worms
Shrimp

'Yuuuuucccccck! What is that?' Max and
Dad have headed closer to the sea on
their rock pool exploration. 'It looks like
a giant underwater sausage!' says Max.

34

Mum, Chelsea and I hurry over to them to see what it is.

Mum laughs when she sees what all the fuss is about. 'It's a sea cucumber, Max. Look, you can pick them up.' She reaches in and carefully lifts the soft, brown, cucumber-like creature from the water. Curly sniffs at it curiously. As he does, it squirts long strands of white, sticky glue from one end. We all scream and jump back. Curly barks at it.

'In some countries they eat these as a special treat,' says Dad, and Mum nods in agreement.

I glance over at Chelsea who looks a little pale and is backing away.

'We're not going to eat it, are we Mr Fletcher?'

'Of course not, Chelsea,' I laugh, 'but this guy is getting his own page in my Vet Diary!'

SEA CUCUMBERS:

- Sea cucumbers are the rubbish collectors of the sea – they clean the surface of the sand as they move along.

- There are 1,250 known species.

- When threatened, sea cucumbers discharge sticky threads.

- They are eaten by lots of fish and sea creatures, and some humans.

I am still sitting working on my 'sea cucumber' page when I hear a low rattling sort of sound behind me. I look around the rocks, but I can't see where it's coming from. Chelsea is a little way off, still recovering from the thought of people eating sea cucumbers.

'Did you hear that, Chelsea?'

'Yeah, what was it?'

We are both quiet and listen again for the sound between the waves lapping on the rocks.

'It's coming from over there,' says Chelsea, pointing to the shelf of rocks behind me.

We carefully creep towards the sound and find ourselves holding

hands as we peer over a large rock.
There, half in a rock pool, is a pelican,
and it's in a lot of trouble!

'Mum! Mum! Come quickly!'

Mum, Dad and Max start to head
towards us as fast as they can across
the slippery rocks. When they reach
us, we all peer over at the very sad
pelican.

'It's caught up in fishing line,' says
Dad.

Mum knows what to do straight
away. Vets always do.

'Juliet and Chelsea, can you run
back to the camp and get some scissors
and some beach towels? We'll have
to try to cut him free before the tide
comes back in.' She looks over at Dad.
'I should have brought my vet kit.'

Chelsea and I look at each other
then race off to the camp site.

We are back in no time and,
of course, I have my vet kit, my
emergency rescue kit, and my pet
carrier too – just in case.

Mum slowly slides down the rocks

beside the pelican. He's very frightened and makes low squawking noises. I snap open my kit on the rocks above our patient. We pass Mum the towels. She's going to have to put them over the bird's head to keep him calm and still while we untangle him. Pelicans are quite big and strong and can give a nasty bite.

When the towels are on, Dad slides down to hold the bird still. Chelsea and I climb down to them and I pass Mum the scissors from my kit and some antiseptic cream. Mum smiles at me. 'Good thinking, Juliet. It's great that you brought your kit.'

'Well, you just have to when you're

nearly a vet,' replies Chelsea.

Mum carefully snips at the line caught around the pelican while I dab along behind her with some antiseptic cream on a cotton ball where the skin has been broken. Luckily he hasn't been cut too badly, but we got here just in time. Had the tide come in, he would have drowned for sure.

Finally the line is all cut away and Mum tells us to get back up on the rocks. She slowly takes the towel off the pelican and for a minute he just stares at us. Then he flaps his wings madly and jumps to the side. We all back away to give him some more space. The pelican flies about ten metres away then lands and looks back at us. Then he starts to clean himself.

'That's a good sign,' says Mum. 'Really sick animals don't bother to clean themselves.'

I must remember to write that in my Vet Diary.

'What is that smell?' asks Dad, and we all look behind us to see Curly wagging his tail. He's found his mullet and he is very, very happy about it. The mullet is looking a little worse for wear. It's now swollen with bulging eyes.

Dad and Chelsea look like they are going to be sick.

'Phew! It stinks!' laughs Max hysterically.

Mum takes charge. 'Girls, I'll get the fish off Curly and you take him up to the camp and wash around his mouth. Dad and I will bury this fish once and for all.'

'I'll help,' says Max, rushing to get his sandcastle spade.

As we drag Curly back to the camp site we try to cover his eyes so he can't see where the fish is being buried. He is very upset about being parted from his treasure again and struggles to break free. I look back at the beach and see that Max is already waist-deep in a hole and still digging.

'Maybe a bath might calm him down,' Chelsea suggests, and ducks into the tent to get her grooming kit.

In no time at all Chelsea has
Curly in a lovely foamy mass and he
does seem to forget his troubles as
she massages the shampoo into his
back and ears. She rinses and trims,
brushes and fluffs, until Curly looks
like a new dog.

'You really do have a gift, Chelsea,'
I say, and Mum nods in agreement as
she comes up from the beach.

Mum and Dad need a rest so we
hang around the camp site after lunch.
Chelsea and I make some posters for
around the campground to educate
people on the dangers of leaving
fishing line lying around. Education is
all part of a vet's job, you know.

CHAPTER
5

Sometimes vets need to be a bit sneaky!

After we've finished putting our posters up, we race down to join Mum, Dad and Max, who are back at the beach.

There are heaps of people down there and a lot of them seem to be doing a funny sort of dance. We can see Mum and Max doing it, too.

'What are you doing?' I pant when we get to them.

'Fishing for pipis!' says Max, proudly holding up his bucket with a dozen or more smooth brown pods of two shells joined together. 'Watch this!' Max puts a pipi on the wet sand and we stare in amazement as the shell opens slightly, flips up onto its end and starts to twist and bury into the sand.

'You find them by twisting your feet into the wet sand.' Mum shows us the action.

Chelsea and I join in and pretty soon we are adding to Max's collection. I look around and notice the fishermen from yesterday are doing it, too.

'Why is everyone collecting them?' I ask, and stop twisting as soon as I hear the answer.

'Some do it for fun, like us,' says
Mum. 'Other people use them for bait.
They pry the shell open with a knife
and put the pipi on the fishing hook.
Fish love them.'

Chelsea, Max and I look down at
our shiny pipis in the bucket. Max
starts to look a bit upset. 'I don't want
my pipis to die.'

'I have an idea, Max,' I whisper.
'Let's take them up to the beach on
the other side of the rock pools and
let them go there where nobody will
find them.'

We all agree that it's a good plan
and Mum wraps her towel around
the bucket so that people don't notice,

otherwise they might follow us for an easy catch.

Curly is excited and runs ahead. He loves an adventure.

We tip the pipis out and sit around them in a circle as they start to burrow. We are taking turns to guess which one will be the last to disappear when suddenly we are greeted by a familiar smell.

'Oh, no!' laughs Mum. 'He's found his mullet again!'

Sure enough Curly, now covered in wet sand, is holding the treasured mullet in his mouth. Its head is now hanging half off and one eye is missing. He wags his tail at us.

Chelsea lets out a small cry. 'Oh Curly, your beautiful coat is filthy again!'

Mum tries to grab the fish off him, but Curly thinks it's a game. He runs around in happy circles, then takes off up the beach towards our tent. Everyone knows who he's going to give it to!

'Dad!' we all screech and run after him, but we're too late.

We hear Dad's bellow a few moments later. Then we see him chasing Curly around the tent with a rolled-up newspaper. Dad is out of breath when we get there.

'That dog . . .' he says to Mum. 'That *dog* just dropped a rotten, stinking mullet on my bare chest while I was asleep. Why he had to come camping, I will never know!'

Chelsea and I try to block Curly's ears. It's not his fault that he likes to fetch things. He usually gets a pat for it.

Dad makes us tie Curly up while he

puts the dead fish in a plastic bag, and then another, and ties them off. He throws the mullet into the wheelie bin on his way to the shower. Dad's not a huge fan of animals, and especially not dead ones by the looks of it.

Curly lets out a little whimper. He liked that mullet.

CHAPTER 6

Vets are always learning

The next morning we are at the beach early and it's a beautiful day. There are surfers out on their boards and the sun is making the water sparkle. Max and Dad are out swimming when everyone starts to call and point out to sea.

There's a pod of dolphins diving through the waves chasing schools of fish. The surfers are so lucky! They're sitting on their boards right amongst them. I would love to be out there, too.

We watch them for ages and then Chelsea and I go back to building the perfect dinosaur zoo out of sand for the dinosaurs Max has carried down to the beach. Mum is reading her book under the umbrella.

After a while one of the surfers comes up the beach to get his stuff right near Mum.

'You were lucky to be out there amongst the dolphins,' says Mum.

'We sure were,' smiles the surfer. 'I haven't seen that many at one time in ages. It must be all the whitebait that's around. There's some pilot whales out there, too, and one of them has a calf.'

He shakes water from his afro, then he dries himself off and heads up the beach with his board under his arm.

By now Chelsea and I are on our feet again, peering out to sea. 'Pilot whales! I've never seen a real whale, Mum. Will we be able to see them from here?'

'I don't think so,' says Mum. 'They don't tend to come in as far as the dolphins. You know, Juliet, pilot whales are not actually whales. They are the second-largest member of the dolphin family, after killer whales.'

I race to my backpack and whip out my Vet Diary, brushing the sand off my hands as I go. This definitely needs a whole page.

PILOT WHALE FACTS:

- Pilot whales are usually dark black, but sometimes they are grey.

- They mostly eat squid and sometimes eat fish.

- Male pilot whales are about 5 metres long.

- There are two species: the long-finned and the short-finned pilot whale.

- Pilot whales aren't really whales at all! They're a type of dolphin.

We head up for lunch and Chelsea and I go over to the toilet block. Curly follows along, but stops at the wheelie bin area. He sniffs and looks around sadly.

'He really liked that mullet,' says

Chelsea, and she bends down to give him a hug.

'Would you like us to groom you to take your mind off it?' she asks him.

Curly tries to lick her cheek and wags his tail. We guess that means yes.

After lunch we play some board games. Curly is looking very smart because Chelsea and I have brushed his hair into sections and made little pigtails all over him.

'That should keep the knots out for a while, anyway,' says Chelsea, leaning over to pat him. Curly seems to be very interested in Max this afternoon. He keeps sniffing around him and laying his head on his lap.

'He just loves me,' laughs Max, as Curly burrows his nose into him again.

Chelsea, Max, Curly and I decide to head back down to the rock pools and hunt for some more sea cucumbers. Mum and Dad sit up at the top of the beach to keep an eye on us.

We find eight sea cucumbers and put them all in one rock pool and start giving them names. I grab my Vet Diary to keep a list so we don't forget them all.

SEA CUCUMBER NAMES:
Chubby
Stretchy
Sticky
Slimy
Blobby
Longy
Stinky (Max named that one)
Bendy

They are the funniest things I have ever felt. They are like long, water-filled balloons that go all floppy when you pick them up. We carry them gently so they don't squirt their glue out because it's really gross and sticky.

Eventually we put our 'pet cucumbers' back where we got them from and head up the beach to Mum and Dad. Then we all head back to the camp site.

Curly runs ahead of us and starts barking like mad when he gets there.

'You guys wait here a minute,' says Dad. He and Mum go ahead to look.

CHAPTER 7

Vets need to know how to follow a trail

'It's okay,' calls Mum after a minute or so. 'You can come now.'

Our camp site is a mess. The plastic bag that held our rubbish has been ripped open and garbage is spread out everywhere.

'Something's got into the garbage,' says Dad. He looks over at Curly.

'Unless Curly has grown some very sharp claws, and leaves rather odd tracks in the sand. I think he's innocent,' says Mum. 'What we have here is the leftovers of a goanna's breakfast. Look – you can see the marks from his tail in the sand. It's a big one.'

'I should have put the garbage in the bin,' says Dad. 'I forgot.'

'What's a goanna?' asks Max.

I whip out my Vet Diary ready to take notes.

'Well, Max, a goanna is actually a relative of your favourite animals . . . the dinosaurs.'

I scribble down as many notes as I can while Mum speaks.

FACTS ABOUT GOANNAS
(also known as monitor lizards):

• They eat meat, including small animals and dead things.

• There are lots of different kinds of goannas and they vary in size. Some grow up to 2m in length.

• They can run fast.

• They can climb trees.

• Goannas can be aggressive if attacked or chased.

I look over at Chelsea. She is now sitting on the table with her legs tucked up, looking around nervously. 'That must have been what we heard the other day in the grass. It could have attacked us!'

'Don't worry, Chelsea. I'm sure it will leave us alone, if we leave it alone.' I look at Mum and she nods.

'And I bet that's what ate all the sausages. Sorry, Curly,' says Dad. Curly wags his tail and looks towards the bin.

'Can we see if we can find it?' says Max. 'I want to see a goanna.'

'I don't,' says Dad. 'Leave it alone.'

'I'll follow the trails with you, Max,' says Mum.

63

Max runs off to grab some dinosaurs from the tent. 'He might want to meet these guys,' he says.

Chelsea and I roll our eyes.

'Do you want to see if we can find it, Chelsea?'

'Um, you know, I'm a bit tired from last night. I might just pop into the tent and read my book.'

'Okay,' I say. 'We'll call you if we see it.'

Chelsea climbs into the tent and zips it shut. I think she put her bag in front of the zip, too.

Mum, Max and I head off. It's really exciting following the strange trails in the sand, but a bit scary, too. Even vets can be scared of new things.

The tracks disappear when we reach the long grass. We all look around, but it's Mum who spots it. 'There it is!' she whispers, pointing up a large gum tree. 'It *is* a beauty.'

I step a little closer to Mum as I look at the enormous lizard with its long tongue flicking in and out.

I'm glad it wasn't what I saw when I opened the tent that first night!

The goanna's green and black markings help camouflage it in the dappled light coming through the trees.

Max holds each of his dinosaurs up for the goanna to see. He insists on giving a description of each one. The lizard looks totally bored. No surprises there.

Finally we head back to camp for our last night. It has been a lovely holiday and I know so much more about beach animals now. I take a bit of time to finish off some pages in my Vet Diary.

CHAPTER
8

Vets have to be good in an emergency!

The next morning we wake up really early because there's heaps of noise coming from the beach. When we come out of the tent, Dad tells us that Mum is already down there because a pilot whale calf has beached itself.

Oh, no! It's probably the one the surfer was talking about yesterday.

'Mum's just sent up a message for us to bring as many buckets as we can. Take these down with you, girls, and I'll wake Max up.'

We run down to the beach and can't believe our eyes! There is a whale lying on the beach and it can't move. It's so awful I feel like crying. Mum is there and we run to her side with the buckets.

'Quickly, girls, help the other people bring buckets of water up. We have to keep her wet and cool or the heat from the sun will kill her.'

Mum turns to a lady who is watching with one hand over her mouth. Mum is very calm. Vets have to be. 'Could you go and get as many beach umbrellas as you can and towels to put over her?'

The woman is glad to be given

something to do and runs up to the camp site. More and more people are coming with buckets and soon we have a line with buckets being passed from one person to the next and the water is gently poured over the whale.

'Will she be all right, Mum?' I start to feel tight in my throat. 'Is she going to be all right?'

'She's been here since last night when the tide was high,' says Mum. 'Her only chance is if we can keep her cool and wet until the tide comes in this afternoon, and then hope that she can find her mother.'

I feel even sadder knowing it is a baby. Its mother must be frantic.

I look out to sea and start to worry.
It's such a big place to look for someone.

The calf blows hard through its
blowhole and opens and closes its
mouth a few times. Its sad little eye
looks up at us.

Chelsea pats her. 'Its going to be
okay,' she whispers to the baby whale.

Suddenly the surfer we saw yesterday

appears at Mum's side. He has run all the way up the beach.

'The pod,' he pants, out of breath. 'They're still out there. We just saw them. They're still after the whitebait.'

Mum looks relieved. 'How long will it be until the tide comes back up to this point?'

'About five hours, I think. It was high

tide around midnight, so it will be high tide again around lunchtime.'

Mum and I look at each other. Vets know what other vets are thinking. That is a long time for the baby whale to stay alive out of the water, and a long time for the pod of pilot whales to stick around. I hope her mother knows we are trying to help.

CHAPTER 9

Sometimes vets need to think fast

Dad brings Mum her mobile phone and she calls Sea World on the Gold Coast and speaks to a marine biologist. He says we are doing everything right. They will try to get here as soon as they can, but they're at least three hours away.

I look at the line of people passing the water. In this heat, they are going to get very tired, very soon. I have an idea and talk it over with Chelsea.

'That's brilliant, Juliet,' she says. 'No wonder you're nearly a vet!'

We make up a roster and go along the line and ask everyone for their name. Then we go up to the camp site and Dad helps us to ask everyone if they could pitch in. If everyone helps, then everyone gets a break, and the baby whale will stay cool and wet until the tide comes back up.

We keep pouring water over the little whale and sheltering her from the hot sun. Every now and then she thrashes about and makes a shrill, panicked sound. I hope her mother can hear her so she doesn't swim away.

Max joins the line of bucket carriers.

I see Mum talking to Dad quietly off to the side. I know she is very worried about the whale.

Ever so slowly, the tide starts to come in. Max uses one of his dinosaurs to mark the highest point a wave reaches each time, and as the scorching sun beats down on us all we wait, and wait, and wait.

By ten o'clock the first wave reaches out from the ocean and touches the whale.

By eleven o'clock we stand around her with the water above our ankles. The whale flips and splashes, but she is still stranded by her weight.

By twelve o'clock it starts to happen.

She starts to be lifted by the waves. The experts from Sea World are here now and the excitement has grown. Our new friend Brett, the surfer, has come back several times to tell us the pod is still out there, and that the mother whale is calling her calf.

'Now,' says the marine biologist to the people gathered around the

three-metre-long baby, 'when the next wave lifts her, we have to try to push her into the deeper water. She will be wonky, so we must try to keep her upright and pointing into the waves so she doesn't roll.'

We all hold our breaths and wait for the next big wave.

'Now,' yells the biologist, and the

whale is pushed forward into the deeper water. The people from Sea World swim out with her and help her through the waves. We are all holding hands and cheering as the little calf slips through the last wave and out to sea.

Brett is waving madly from his board. He signals that the whales are heading in the right direction and he puts his thumbs up when the mother reaches her calf.

The whole beach cheers and every face is smiling.

We stagger up to our camp site and collapse onto the chairs. The people from Sea World are going to stay on for a while, to make sure more whales don't beach themselves.

Mum looks exhausted, but happy. 'Well, you did say you wanted to see a pilot whale, Juliet!'

I look around for Curly to give him a hug. I haven't seen him all morning.

'Dad, where's Curly?'

'I thought he was with you?'

None of us have seen him for ages.

We all start to call out for him.

I start to panic. We were so caught up with the whale that nobody kept an eye on Curly.

'Curly! Curly!' I bellow.

We run around the camp site asking if anyone has seen him. The lady in the tent next door remembers giving him a biscuit around morning tea time, but there are no reports since then.

'Oh where could he be?' I sob.

Max, Chelsea and I are all crying now, and Mum and Dad look really worried too. What a terrible way to end our holiday! First the whale, now this!

A huge garbage truck is coming up the dirt path to collect the wheelie bins. He honks his horn for us to hop off the track. Can't he see we are freaking out? He honks again. I look up to signal for him to stop so I can tell him that our dog is missing. Then I see a very familiar face looking out of the window at me.

It's Curly, still covered in little pigtails.

The driver stops his truck and lifts Curly down. 'Are you looking for this?' he laughs when we run over.

Max, Chelsea and I all hug Curly. He doesn't know who to lick first.

'I saw him in my rear-view mirror following the truck while I collected the bins,' says the driver, 'so I thought I'd better bring him back. With a hairdo like that, he obviously belonged to someone!'

Chelsea looks very proud.

'We should have guessed. He followed the mullet!' says Dad, shaking his head and laughing.

It takes ages to pack all the gear up and sweep the sand out of the tent.

When we are finally finished we all go
down to the beach for one last swim.
As I jump in the waves I look out to
sea and smile at the thought of the
whale calf back with its mother.

'You know,' says Dad, when we are back in the car and driving home, 'I'm sure I can still smell that dead fish.'

Mum shakes her head and smiles.

Chelsea and I give Curly a hug.

Max puts his hand in his pocket and pulls out a pet pipi he's been saving from two days ago.

Curly barks excitedly as the smell fills the car.

Juliet
nearly a
Vet

Zookeeper for a Day

CHAPTER 1

Some vets work at zoos

I walk into the kitchen for breakfast and find my brother Max is hogging the whole table with little piles of cereal pieces.

'What *are* you doing, Max?' I ask.

'Playing with my food,' he says. 'It's a new cereal called Dino Snaps. Every piece is a little dinosaur packed full of fibre!'

I roll my eyes. He's obviously used the TV commercial to con Mum into buying them.

'Haven't you got enough dinosaurs without eating them as well?' I say, feeling a bit annoyed.

'She got you some too,' he says, fixing his line of iguanodons.

I sigh as I open the pantry. As if I care what shape my cereal is.

'Ooh, Zoo Snaps!' I say. They're shaped like cute little zoo animals! I turn the box around to look at the back and that's when I see it – *Want to be a zookeeper for a day?* It's a competition where you can win a day at the zoo with a real zookeeper.

I read the entry conditions out loud. 'In twenty-five words or less, tell us why you would make a great zookeeper.'

I whip my Vet Diary out of my back pocket. To be a vet, I have to have had experience with all kinds of animals. This is just what I need!

My best friend Chelsea, who lives next door, comes over just as I am jotting down some ideas.

'Chelsea, I'm going to win a competition where you get to be a zookeeper for a day, and you get to take a friend!' I show her the cereal box.

'That's *sooo* cool,' says Chelsea. 'You'd be perfect for that, Juliet. You're nearly a vet, so you'd be really helpful.'

'And imagine all the animals that would need grooming at a zoo, Chelsea.'

Chelsea frowns. 'I'm not sure about

brushing tigers . . .'

I laugh. 'I don't think they'll put us in with the tigers! Besides, if you're going to be a world-famous animal trainer and groomer one day, you'll have to get used to some tricky animals.'

'Imagine how great it would be?' says Chelsea.

'I know, we just have to win. We can enter as many times as we like, as long as each entry has a barcode from a box of Snaps cereal. Max and I both have one, so that's two entries already!'

We start working on our twenty-five-word entry forms right away.

'How does this sound?' I say after a while.

Sounds good to me,' says Chelsea. 'How many words is it?'

I count. 'Twenty-seven.'

We both look at the page. 'You could say *I'm* instead of *I am*. That would save one word. And maybe just say *ten* instead of *ten years old*. That will give us one word left we can use. How about *please*?'

'Perfect,' I say, and make the changes.

We fill in the two entry forms and walk them to the post box in the next street.

Now all we have to do is wait . . . and eat a whole lot more cereal.

CHAPTER
2

Vets can be disappointed

After weeks of eating *lots* of Zoo Snaps, finally it's the day of the competition draw.

Chelsea and I take the phone into the lounge room and watch animal movies so that we'll be right there when they call.

'Juliet speaking,' I say, when the phone rings at 2.00 p.m. Chelsea nods at me. She has her fingers crossed in her lap.

'Oh, hi Gran,' I say, trying not to

sound too disappointed. 'Mum's at the surgery and I'm waiting for a very important call. Can we call you back later?' I shake my head at Chelsea.

'Okay, Gran, love you too.'

We sit and wait all afternoon, but the phone doesn't ring again.

'I can't believe it,' says Chelsea, as she heads home for dinner. 'I thought we had a really good chance of winning.'

Even though it's Friday night, I go to bed early because I feel really grumpy and Max is annoying me.

The next morning I wake up to a terrible smell. Curly's rolled in chook poo again and he's standing beside my bed wagging his tail. I'm glad Chelsea's coming over. It looks like the first thing we will be doing is bathing Curly. Again.

The phone rings as we are up to our armpits in bubbles and dog hair. I'm holding Curly still in the laundry tub while Chelsea massages special apple-scented dog shampoo into his coat.

Max answers the phone. 'No, she can't come to the phone, she's busy.' He hangs up.

'Who was that Max?' says Mum.

'I don't know,' says Max, lining up his toy dinosaurs across the table. 'Someone wanting Juliet.'

Curly hears Mum's voice and tries

to leap out of the tub, just as the
phone rings again. This time Mum
gets it.

She comes into the laundry with a
big smile on her face. 'Juliet, it's for you.
It's Susan calling from Snaps Cereal.'

I'm so excited that I let go of Curly
and he leaps out of the laundry tub
and runs through the house shaking
and barking. I can hardly hear the

lady on the phone. She tells me that I
HAVE WON!

'We won! They say we can go next
Saturday,' I say to Chelsea and Mum
as soon as I get off the phone. 'We're
going to be zookeepers!' Chelsea and
I jump around the laundry. Mum is
really excited for us too.

'We're going to be so busy getting
our zoo kits ready in time!' I say.

CHAPTER
3

Vets need to make a good impression

'Have you remembered all your different combs?' I say to Chelsea the night before we go. 'There will be heaps of different hair types.'

'Uh-huh,' says Chelsea. 'And I've got a notebook for writing down training tips.'

'Good thinking,' I say.

We go to bed early because we have to be at the zoo at 7 a.m. and it's a long drive. Mum's going to take us, so Chelsea gets to sleep over.

Mum looks at my bulging vet kit as I walk out to the car the next morning.

'You know, Juliet, you won't need that today. The zoo vets will have everything they need.'

'Mum,' I say. 'How many times has my vet kit come in handy? I'm not taking any chances. The reason we won is because they know I'm nearly a vet, so the least they will expect is for me to have my own kit. We're going to impress them with how helpful we can be.'

'Oh, I'm sure you'll make an impression all right,' says Dad as he puts Chelsea's grooming kit into the car.

When we get to the zoo, Mum comes

in with us to sign forms and check when she should pick us up. We're going to be here until 3 p.m! That's seven hours of zoo time!

We start by showing Peter, our zookeeper for the day, our vet kits. He's so impressed he doesn't know what to say. He just looks at Mum with big eyes.

'It's going to be really crazy here today,' he says to Mum. 'Sabula, one of our elephants, is due to have her first calf. The vets have been with her all night and it looks like it's going to happen today.'

'Those vets will have their hands full,' Mum says.

'It's lucky Juliet is here,' says Chelsea.

The keeper looks a bit confused.

'She's nearly a vet,' Chelsea explains.

We kiss Mum goodbye and turn back to Peter. He gives us both a 'Zookeeper for a Day' T-shirt and we race off to put them on.

'Right,' I say when we get back. 'Where do we start?'

Peter tells us that the first thing we will be doing is checking the animals are all safe and well after the night. As he speaks I make a list in my Vet Diary.

ZOOKEEPER JOBS:

• Check on animals after night-time in their inside enclosures.
• Make sure they have no injuries.

Our first stop is the sun bears.

'I didn't realise how much of a zoo you don't see when you visit,' says Chelsea as we walk down the corridors behind all the cages.

The bears are very happy to see Peter. He taps his hand on the wire mesh and one of them stands up and puts her paws against the wire. Her long hooked nails poke through the wire and Chelsea takes a step back.

'Did you know, Chelsea, that they're called sun bears because they have the shape of the sun on their necks?' I say.

Peter nods and gives me a smile. He opens a container on his hip and

scoops out some white gooey stuff
with his fingers.

'Ew, what's that?' yelps Chelsea.
'I don't think I can watch!'

Peter stares at her for a moment.
'It's porridge.'

'Oh,' smiles Chelsea, biting her lip.

Peter puts his fingers up against
the wire and the sun bear licks the
porridge from them.

'Lots of zoo animals are trained to
stand up like this, so we can check
their undersides for injuries. It's called
target training,' he explains, 'and it
gets the animals used to having the
vets treat them without being sedated.'

Chelsea has her notebook out and

is writing furiously. 'I could try that on Princess, my cat,' she says.

I bob down to get a closer look at the bears' tummies as each one stands up. 'They all look fine, Peter,' I say.

Suddenly the door opens and a vet in surgical clothes comes rushing into the room. His name tag says 'Ben'.

'Peter, we need a hand with the giraffes. Kamu has torn his ear overnight and we need the others out of the way. I'm short on time because Sabula could have the calf at any time.'

'Right,' says Peter, and we're off.

CHAPTER
4

Vets should always be prepared

Chelsea and I struggle to keep up as Peter and Ben stride along the path towards the giraffe enclosure.

'Wow, I thought the bears were big!' gasps Chelsea when we get there. 'They are so beautiful up close.'

The giraffes are bunched in a corner. Their long, graceful necks cross over each other as they look at us. The largest one has a small patch of blood on his ear. It's hard to see from all the way down here.

'I don't know what he's cut it on
or how bad it is, but I need to take a
look,' says Ben. 'Can you get the others
down the end and we'll try to get
Kamu into the crush?'

'Sure,' says Peter, and we trot off
after him.

'Why would they want to crush
him?' whispers Chelsea.

'A crush is a special narrow pen
where they can stop the animal from
moving around, Chelsea,' Peter says,
laughing. She looks very relieved.

Peter grabs some carrots and
climbs up to a tall platform. 'You can
come up with me,' he calls down, 'but
one at a time.'

'You go up, Chelsea,' I say. 'I want to watch the vet.'

I walk back to where some other keepers are helping to separate Kamu from the giraffes and herd him into a small pen. I can't help but peek into Ben's vet kit lying open on the ground. It's very impressive and has instruments I haven't seen in Mum's surgery. I might need to get myself some new supplies.

I hear Chelsea giggling and look over to see her on the high platform with Peter, feeding carrots to the giraffes. Their long blue tongues wrap around the carrots and pull them into their mouths. 'Ew yuk!' she squeaks, as giraffe slobber drips on her shorts. She won't be happy about that.

Ben has climbed to the platform beside the crush and is now looking at Kamu's ear. Another keeper is feeding carrots to the patient and a vet nurse stands by to pass equipment up to Ben.

'Ah, I see what the problem is,' says Ben to the nurse below. 'He's got a huge splinter. He must have been rubbing his head against the trees or something. Can you pass me my tweezers, please?'

The vet nurse looks around in the kit. 'Can you remember where you put them? They're not in the usual spot.'

'Oh, blast. I left them in the steriliser after I stitched that water buffalo. Can you run and get them?'

'I have tweezers!' I say, throwing my vet kit open. 'And I sterilised them in my mum's surgery just before we came.'

They all look over, as if noticing me for the first time.

'I'm Juliet,' I say, shrugging. 'I'm nearly a vet.'

'Well, Juliet, *nearly* a vet,' says the vet nurse, smiling, 'you'd better take your sterile tweezers up to Ben, *really* a vet.'

I cannot believe my luck! I told mum my vet kit would come in handy. I just knew it. I can't get the smile off my face as I climb the ladder and pass the vet my tweezers.

I'm about to climb down when Ben says, 'You can't leave now. This could end up being a two-vet job, you know!'

I look over at Chelsea brushing a giraffe's neck and give her a tiny wave and a huge smile. Right now, all our dreams have just come true.

Ben carefully pulls out the large splinter (I'm allowed to keep it!) and I dab some antiseptic cream on Kamu's ear before we climb down the ladder.

I proudly return my tweezers to my kit and put the splinter in a specimen jar, then I snap the kit shut.

'Well, it's a lucky thing we have another vet on duty today,' smiles Ben. 'We might need a hand if this baby elephant decides to finally make an entrance today.' He ruffles my hair, picks up his kit and heads off.

'I can't wait to be a real vet,' I whisper under my breath.

'Okay,' says Peter, appearing beside me. 'We'd better clean out these enclosures before we let the animals out of their night stalls. The zoo will open soon and the visitors aren't going to like it if all they can see are piles of dung.'

I whip out my diary and turn to the page of zookeeper jobs.

ZOOKEEPER JOBS:

• Check on animals after night-time in their inside enclosures.
• Make sure they have no injuries.
• Pick up dung.

Peter hands us each a scoop and
a bucket as we enter the red panda
enclosure. The panda looks at us
through the bars of its night cage as
we walk around scooping up droppings.
Peter follows us, raking the sand.

'Chelsea, if you keep holding your
breath, you're going to faint!' I laugh.

She says nothing, but she shakes
her head quickly. It's hard to speak
when your cheeks are full of air.

'I know,' says Peter to the gorgeous
panda as it looks out at us. 'We're a bit
late with breakfast this morning, but
the girls are going to get it for you as
soon as we're finished.'

I grab a specimen jar out of my vet

kit and use a stick to poke some red panda poo into it.

I look up to see Peter staring at me with an odd look on his face.

'I have a scat collection,' I explain. 'I have droppings from twenty-three different animals already at home. You know, you can learn an awful lot about an animal from its poo.'

'Well, I've never met one like you before,' says Peter, shaking his head. I smile. I think he likes me.

CHAPTER
5

Zoo animals eat a lot!

We head into the zoo kitchen and it is super busy. The amount of food that is being cut up is incredible.

Peter can see we're amazed. There are huge tubs of fruit, vegetables, pellets and grain spread out around us, and each staff member is carefully reading clipboards and weighing amounts of food before putting them into labelled trays.

'Will they eat all of this in one week?' I ask.

'Oh, no,' laughs Peter. 'This is just for one day! There's also a meat locker for all the carnivores and an insect room where the maggots, mealworms, crickets and other insects are raised.'

I whip out my Vet Diary as Peter keeps talking.

ZOO KITCHEN FACTS:

- More kinds of food are served in a zoo than in most restaurants.

- Zoos buy huge amounts of grain, fruit, vegetables, meat, fish, and other foods. In one year this zoo uses 19,000 eggs and 54,000 carrots.

- Some animals are picky eaters in nature and need special diets. A famous example is the koala, which eats only the fresh leaves of eucalyptus trees.

- Many animals eat their food as it comes, but some need their food measured, chopped, combined, or even cooked.

'I'm going to leave you girls here to help prepare some meals for the animals while I go and finish raking and cleaning enclosures,' says Peter.

'Oh, hang on, Peter,' I say, reaching for some specimen jars from my vet kit. 'Can you get me some more scat samples, please?'

Peter looks at me for a minute, then smiles and takes the jars. I bet he's going to want to start his own scat collection now I've given him the idea.

'Please don't make me touch a maggot, Juliet,' whispers Chelsea in my ear.

Chelsea and I help the zoo staff with preparing the food for the red panda, penguins, sun bears, tamarins, otters, iguanas and the bamboo partridges. I make a page for each in my diary for when we go to visit them so I can write down any facts.

Whilst Chelsea cuts the fruit and vegetables into very neat little pieces, I go with a lady called Stacey to the room where all the insects are being bred.

The smell is disgusting! I pull a face and slap my hand over my mouth. It's lucky that Chelsea didn't come too.

'Gotta get used to bad smells if you want to work with animals,' says Stacey gruffly. We scoop some mealworms (which are not actually worms at all, but beetle larvae) into little dishes and collect some fly pupae (these are maggots in cocoons turning into flies!). We also grab a couple of containers of crickets.

'Not many animals actually like maggots,' says Stacey as I peer into the tank full of writhing white fly larvae, 'but lots of them love the pupae.'

I couldn't imagine eating anything worse.

As we come out of the insect room, a man returns with a large tub of porridge.

'Did she eat anything?' asks Stacey.

'No,' says the big man. 'Ben hopes she's not far off now, so fingers crossed. She's having a lot of trouble.'

Chelsea and I know they are talking about the baby elephant being born. 'Imagine if we got to see a newborn elephant calf!' I say.

Stacey overhears me. 'They won't let you anywhere near that calf today. The public won't see it till the end of the week.' She walks back into the insect room.

'We're not the public!' says Chelsea. 'Juliet, you're nearly a vet. You've already helped out once today.'

Peter comes back in and we load up our cart to go and feed some animals.

I really hope we do get to see the baby elephant if it's born soon.

Our first stop is the tamarin

monkeys. They are so cute and little. Peter lets us come in with him and we sit quietly on the ground. The little monkeys know Peter and climb straight up onto his shoulders. He passes them mealworms and they gobble them down like chocolates. Chelsea screws up her nose, but smiles.

A young tamarin creeps over and sits at our feet.

'Hold your hands out flat and put some peas on them,' says Peter quietly. I slowly put my hand into the dish and hold it out with a small pile of peas. The little monkey holds my thumb with his tiny hand and pops the peas into his mouth, watching us the whole time.

'He's so cute,' whispers Chelsea.

'We'd better keep moving,' says Peter. 'There are lots of hungry mouths to feed!' He fills their bowls with clean water and fresh food.

'Can you grab a box of crickets from the cart, Juliet,' he says. 'We'll let them go in here to give these little guys something to hunt. It's really important to keep zoo animals busy so they don't get bored.'

I grab the crickets and pull the lid off just as a monkey leaps past and knocks the box from my hand. Crickets leap in every direction, including into Chelsea's hair!

The monkeys go crazy chasing the crickets around. Chelsea goes crazy too.

'Juliet! Juliet! They're in my hair!' she gasps, frantically trying to sweep the crickets off as they scurry for a hiding spot. 'Get them off! Get them off!'

Peter and I do our best to get them all off her, but she is still a little shaken

when we leave the pen. Her hair is the messiest I've ever seen it.

'Oh dear,' whimpers Chelsea. 'I don't like crickets. I really don't like crickets. Can you see any more in my hair?'

'It's okay now, Chelsea,' I soothe, trying my best to fix her hair. Chelsea always has really, really neat hair.

'They're all gone and your hair looks fine, doesn't it, Peter?'

'Sure,' says Peter, nodding his head and trying not to smile.

Next we visit the red panda again. Peter fills her bowls and we help tie flowers and bamboo to the trees. I scribble a few quick notes:

RED PANDA FOOD:
- berries
- flowers
- bamboo
- eggs

Then we're off to the bamboo partridge enclosure. We sprinkle seeds, nuts, grapes, diced fruit and a few mealworms on the ground. The pretty brown and tan birds scurry around to eat them. Peter hangs some orange halves in the trees for them to find.

The animals' food looks so fresh and lovely that my tummy starts to rumble. It must be nearly time for morning tea. Zookeepers work really hard.

CHAPTER
6

Vets need to eat too

We push our cart around the path behind Peter, stopping every now and then to feed the animals on our list. There are so many creatures at the zoo and each keeper is responsible for cleaning and feeding different ones. Peter has to feed even more today because extra people are helping with the baby elephant birth.

Next we throw lettuce into the iguana enclosure. Max would love these guys, because the huge lizards really do look like living dinosaurs.

'Otters and penguins are next,' says Peter, 'and then we'll stop for some morning tea.'

To feed the otters, Peter has to put on long rubber pants called waders and a big coat and gloves. It's really slippery in there and Peter tells us that otters might look very cute, but they have sharp teeth and can give a nasty bite. He takes a bucket of crayfish in and hides them amongst the rocks. The otters scurry around poking their little black faces with long whiskers into all the rock crevices.

'That should keep them busy for a

while,' he says as he comes back out.

The Australian little penguins are next door, and this time we're allowed to come in. Peter shows us how to hold the tiny dead fish by the tail so that they go down the penguins' throats headfirst. They love them and crowd around us like little men in fancy suits.

'I can't believe we're doing this!' I say to Chelsea. 'It was *soooo* worth eating all that cereal!'

'Hey, Mum, look at that!'

A boy with an ice-cream is looking over the fence at us. Chelsea and I laugh and wave. It feels very cool being on the other side of the fence.

'Hey, what's wrong with my fish?'
Chelsea asks. The penguins look at
it as she dangles it over their beaks,
then they turn away.

'It's because it's bent,' laughs Peter.
'These penguins are very picky with

the fish they eat. They won't eat any fish that are bent or damaged.'

'I think they might be a bit spoilt,' sniffs Chelsea, and I think she might be right. She does know a lot about training animals.

We wash the fish from our fingers and I make a quick couple of notes.

PENGUIN FOOD FACTS:

- Penguins like to eat their fish headfirst so the fins don't get stuck in their throats.

- They don't like their fish to be bent or damaged.

For morning tea, Peter takes us to the animal enrichment area. This is where they make things to keep the animals entertained.

'A bored animal is an unhealthy animal,' I explain to Chelsea.

We make some toys for the animals as we eat our snacks. Peter goes off to check on the elephant.

The first thing we make is for the capuchin monkeys. Leisa, another zookeeper, shows us how to put walnuts into the bottom of plastic containers and cover the tops with masking tape.

'The monkeys will use the rocks in their enclosures to break through the tape,' she explains, 'and then they eat the nuts.'

'Animals are so clever,' says Chelsea. I agree.

We start on the toys for the bears. They love to rummage and hunt for their food, so we help Leisa hide food in their toys. It's great fun. Mine look a bit messy when we're finished, but Chelsea's are all very colourful and neat. I wonder if the bears will notice the difference.

I make a list in my diary of the things we've made, so I can tell Mum later.

THINGS TO KEEP BEARS FROM GETTING BORED:

- Plastic bottles with grapes and raisins in them.

- Hard plastic plumbing pipes with coconuts full of porridge inside.

- Hollow bamboo stalks stuffed with dry biscuits.

- Pine cones smeared with sticky treats like peanut butter or honey.

- Hollow plastic toys filled with treats and frozen into popsicles.

- Hard plastic balls smeared with peanut butter or jam for them to lick off.

When Peter comes back from the elephant area, he looks worried.

'She's really struggling,' he says to Leisa. 'I think they're getting pretty concerned.' The zookeepers talk for a while in low voices and I try to listen.

'Oh no, Juliet!' Chelsea startles me when she whispers in my ear. She sounds quite upset.

'I'm sure the elephant and her calf will be fine,' I tell her.

'It's not that. I think I have a cricket in my shirt still. It's driving me crazy. I can feel it. Will you have a look?'

We duck off to the toilet and I look in Chelsea's shirt. 'I'm sure you're just imagining it,' I say when I see

137

nothing there. 'Remember when Bertie Brownstone had head lice and you washed your hair six times in one night? It'll be just like that. There are no crickets on you, I promise.'

When we come out, Peter is waiting for us.

'Boy, have I got a job for you two,' he says.

I run to grab my kit. 'Come on, Chelsea!' I say. 'It might be time to brush that tiger!'

CHAPTER 7

Vets need a lot of help

'It's time to scrub a tortoise,' says Peter.

'Now that sounds like fun,' says Chelsea, grabbing her grooming kit.

Peter takes us to the grassy area where the huge Galápagos tortoises roam around nibbling the grass.

'This is Grandpa,' he says. 'He's 142 years old!'

Chelsea and I fall in love with Grandpa immediately. He's huge! Peter tells us some facts about him and I write them down.

GRANDPA THE GALAPAGOS TORTOISE:

• Grandpa weighs just under 400kg.

• He is 1.5m long!

• He has been at the zoo since it opened and originally came from the London Zoo.

• Grandpa's very friendly.

'Now,' says Peter, 'Grandpa here is getting a bit too old to go for swims in the pond these days, and we like to keep his shell nice and clean for him. Do you think you could give him a bit of a scrub?'

'Are you kidding?' I laugh. 'Chelsea is nearly a world-famous animal trainer and groomer. We'll have

Grandpa looking shiny in no time.'

'I thought you might,' Peter smiles. 'Here's a bucket of lettuce and fruit for Grandpa. If you put this in front of him he'll stay nice and still for you. I've got to go and do some more cleaning jobs, but Marcia is just over there,' he points to a lady trimming a hedge, 'and she can radio if you need me.'

'Thanks, Peter,' we say together.

'I bet he's going to check on the elephant,' I say as he walks off. 'I think there's a problem. Vets have a special sense for these things.'

'They'll look after her,' says Chelsea. 'Come on, let's get busy!' She snaps open her kit on the grass.

We scrub and rub and clean and scrape. We use toothbrushes to get into all the tight places and steel wool to buff up the dry, flaky spots. Chelsea even gives Grandpa a manicure. He loves it and just keeps on munching. Every now and then he stretches his neck up really tall and looks around.

GRANDPA

'He's doing that because he wants his neck washed as well,' says Chelsea. We do a great job on that too.

Chelsea takes some rags out of her kit and finally we polish his shell.

When Peter comes back he is amazed. 'Wow,' he says. 'Grandpa has never looked so clean. He looks eighty years younger!'

Marcia comes over to have a look too. They are both very impressed, especially with the lovely blue ribbon we Blu Tacked to his shell.

'Ready to go and feed some babies?' Peter asks us.

Could this day get any better? We gather our kits and head to the animal nursery. It's not even lunchtime yet and we're both exhausted, but there's no way we want to stop for a rest.

When Peter takes us into the nursery we have to be really quiet. There are a few cages with some sick animals in them, but I am pleased that most of them are empty. One of the cages has a large, colourful bird in it. It doesn't look well. The vet nurse is giving it some medicine from a dropper.

'That's a macaw,' says Peter. 'He's a bit sick at the moment, but Sophie will get him back on the mend.' Sophie looks over and gives us a smile and motions that we can come closer.

'I'm Juliet,' I whisper.

'She's nearly a vet,' says Peter. 'And this is Chelsea. She's nearly an animal trainer and groomer.'

'Well, how lucky that you're here,' says Sophie. 'We're short-staffed today and I could use some help from people with experience.'

'What can we help with?' I say, as I pop open my kit.

'Well,' says Sophie, clearly impressed, 'as soon as I've finished this job I need to bathe a very dirty little Tasmanian devil and then entertain some cheeky baby meerkats. Do either of those jobs interest you?'

Our eyes must nearly pop out of our heads because Peter and Sophie burst out laughing.

CHAPTER 8

Vets have some lovely jobs

Sophie carefully uncovers a tiny little Tasmanian devil that is in a carry crate. It is about the size of a six-week-old puppy and is so cute. He is covered in mud and has some fur missing from his back.

Sophie gently lifts him out of the crate in a towel. He opens his mouth as if to hiss, but no sound comes out. He thinks he's so fierce.

'Now let's have a look at you, Buster,' she says. 'One of the keepers noticed this little joey was extra muddy and had some fur missing. We just want to clean him up and check him for cuts before we give him back to his mum.'

Sophie gets Chelsea and me to prepare a basin of warm water, and she holds Buster while we gently sponge the dirt off his fur. The little devil looks up at us with his small black eyes.

'I'll do the area where the hair is missing,' says Sophie.

She has a closer look at him. 'No cuts. Probably just play fighting with your brothers and sisters,' she says to the little devil. 'Tasmanian devils are pretty tough on each other. It's a battle to survive from the minute they're born.'

We dry him off with a warm towel and wrap him up like a baby. Buster goes to sleep in Chelsea's arms.

Sophie calls another zookeeper to tell her that Buster's fine to go back to his mum, and we put him back into his crate.

'Now,' she says, 'are you ready to meet my ratbags?'

She takes us into another room where there is a playpen on the ground. 'Shhh,' she says as she steps in and motions for us to follow. We sit down on the blanket beside her.

Sophie taps her fingers on the top of a plastic box with a hole in it, and we hear movement inside.

'Watch this,' she says.

All of a sudden three little heads fill the doorway and peep out at us.

'Baby meerkats!' I can hardly control my excitement.

'Come on,' whispers Sophie to the shy babies. 'Come on.' She rolls a tennis ball on the blanket and they all watch it closely.

They are little balls of fluff with grey heads, honey-coloured bodies and long skinny tails. They bounce out across the floor towards the ball and jump all over it, tumbling over the top of each other. Every now and then, one of them tries to stand up on its back legs, then gets bowled over by another. They *really are* the cutest things I have ever seen.

The babies start racing around and climbing onto our legs then leaping off.

'Why are they here?' I ask, as Sophie gently scoops one up and hands it to me.

'Their mum rejected them for some reason. We don't know why, but sometimes that happens in nature.' The little meerkat starts to lick my thumb.

'They're due for a feed,' says Sophie. 'Can you girls play with them while I warm up their bottles? These babies are going to be part of our zoo education program, so they need to get used to people.'

'Will they ever go back in with the other meerkats?'

'I'm afraid not,' says Sophie. 'Meerkats are very territorial and would chase them away and possibly hurt them.'

Sophie returns a minute later with three warm little bottles.

'We've done something like this before,' I say. 'After a bushfire, we had to help my mum. She's a vet. We had to feed a whole lot of orphaned sugar gliders and possums.'

'I knew you girls would be a great help!' Sophie says.

We sit together on the floor and give the baby meerkats their bottles.

Chelsea strokes hers with her finger and we look at each other and smile.

Every so often, Chelsea scratches herself and looks uncomfortable.

'I still think I've got crickets on me,' she whispers.

'No, you haven't,' I say.

Peter comes in and tells us we will be having a special guest join us for lunch.

We thank Sophie, kiss our meerkats goodbye, grab our kits and head off. I knew zoos were busy places, but this is ridiculous!

We walk into a large room with a table set up in front of a large cage. There are some sandwiches on plates for us, but I can only see stools for three people.

'I thought we were having a guest?' says Chelsea.

'You are,' says Peter. 'I'm just getting his lunch.' He walks out of the room and comes back with a very big piece of meat hooked onto a chain. He opens a door in the cage and hangs the meat up on the mesh. Then he locks the cage and speaks to someone on his radio.

CHAPTER 9

Vets get scared too

'Let him in, Tom, we're good to go.'

Chelsea nearly falls off her seat when a huge Sumatran tiger pads into the cage in front of us from a side door. I must admit, for a moment I panic too.

'This is Rabu,' says Peter, 'and he's going to have lunch with us.'

The three of us sit and eat sandwiches while we watch the massive tiger eat his enormous piece of meat. It is the scariest thing I've ever seen, but it's exciting too.

When Rabu's finished, he licks himself, yawns and stretches, then heads back out the door he came in.

'He's going outside for a sleep in the sun,' says Peter.

'They really are just big cats, aren't they?' says Chelsea. 'Princess does that after she eats too.'

'What do we do now?' I say, feeling a little sleepy myself.

'We need to take a load of hay to the zebras and deer,' says Peter. 'Then it will be just about time for your mum to come and get you.'

'In case I forget to tell you later, Peter, we've had the BEST day,' I say.

Chelsea nods in agreement.

As we are loading the hay, I can't help notice that Peter keeps looking towards the elephant house. I can see he's worried, but he doesn't say anything. Vets and zookeepers must get really attached to the animals they care for.

We're allowed to ride on the buggy

with him as it tows the load of hay towards the plains animals' area.

Peter's radio crackles and we hear a man's voice over the motor of the buggy.

'Change of plan,' says Peter, smiling, and he turns the vehicle around.

'Has the baby been born?' I ask.

'Is it okay?' says Chelsea.

'Whoa, slow down!' laughs Peter. 'Let's just go and have a look, hey?'

We stop outside a huge barn and tiptoe inside behind Peter. There are lots of zookeepers there, but they are all watching very quietly. We all stand behind the rails of a massive fence and peer through.

I let out a gasp.

There, on the ground, is a tiny baby elephant. It looks so little compared to its mother. The only movement is its little sausage-like trunk flicking gently up and down.

'The calf is very weak because the mother has had so much trouble having her,' whispers Peter. 'The vets are waiting to see if she'll need help standing up to feed. Her mother will try to help her.'

I hold onto Chelsea's arm. Already you can see how much the mother elephant loves her baby. She runs her enormous trunk over her calf's little body, as if she's checking it's all right.

'Please get up, little one,' whispers a young zookeeper beside me. It feels as if all of us are holding our breath.

The little calf struggles and falls so many times. She just can't seem to do it. The mother elephant tries to help her with her trunk, but the baby keeps slipping and falling. She doesn't have the strength to stand.

She's so beautiful. Her little ears and body are a perfect mini version of her mother. She looks so gorgeous. If only she could stand.

The other elephants are all looking through the bars at her, and like us they are silent and worried.

'Time to step in, I think,' says Ben,

the vet I helped with the giraffes.
He and three other men slowly climb
into the yard. The mother elephant
looks at them warily and swings her
trunk from side to side. She keeps
looking down at her baby.

Peter passes them a large piece of
fabric.

'Good girl, Sabula,' says Ben, as he
walks over to the mother and strokes
her cheek. 'Let us help you get this
baby to her feet.'

The four men gently pass the fabric
under the calf's tummy and hold one
corner each. The mother elephant lays
her trunk on her baby's back. I'm sure
she knows they are trying to help.

When Ben nods they all start to lift,
and slowly she is drawn up to stand.
'Let's hold her for a minute until she
gets her legs steady,' says Ben.

We all stand and wait.

The calf steadies herself then slowly
takes a tiny step, then another. Her
little trunk swings and knots and
twists and pokes. It's like she doesn't
know how to control it, but it's so cute
to watch.

She finds her mother's enormous
face with it and wraps it around the
middle of her mum's trunk. Slowly the
men lower the cloth.

'She's standing by herself!' whispers
Chelsea.

'Now we just need her to drink some milk,' says Peter.

And then, ever so slowly, the little calf shuffles to her mother's side. Her trunk explores and her mouth finally finds what she needs: a long, warm drink of milk.

Ben turns and smiles at the group of teary-eyed onlookers. I turn around to look behind me and I see Mum. I slide past the others and give her a huge hug.

'Well, I think you just saw something most vets will never see,' says Mum quietly, hugging me right back.

A newspaper photographer is let in

to take a photo of the newborn baby, and Ben lets us stand in the photo.

'Is my hair okay?' fusses Chelsea.

'Perfect,' I say. 'You look like a world-famous animal trainer and groomer.'

NEW BABY AT THE ZOO!

'And you look just like a vet!' laughs Chelsea.

In the car on the way home Chelsea and I tell Mum about every single thing we've seen and done today. She is very impressed.

Chelsea is in the middle of telling Mum about the blue ribbon on Grandpa the tortoise when she falls asleep against my shoulder, and there, out of the corner of my eye I see . . . a cricket climbing out of her shirt!

Chelsea was right, there was one in there still!

Juliet
nearly a
Vet

The Lost Dogs

CHAPTER 1

Dogs know vets will help them

I wake up to a scratching noise, but I try to ignore it. There was a storm last night that kept me awake and I just want to go back to sleep.

'Stop it, Max,' I groan and I bury my head under my pillow. Max is my annoying five-year-old brother and he's crazy about dinosaurs. It's all he thinks about. He's probably playing with his dinosaur toys in the hallway again.

The scratching continues and I'm just about to call out for a second time

when I hear a little whimper. That's
not Max, I think, sitting up in bed.
It's coming from outside.

I go to the front door and look out
through the glass. It's a dog. A really
scruffy, skinny-looking dog. I put my
hand up to the glass and the dog licks
at it from the other side. It must know
I'm nearly a vet.

Vets know they have to be careful
about touching stray dogs, but I can
see this one's friendly and needs help.

I open the front door just a little
and the dog pushes its shaggy, brown
and white face inside. Its tongue is out
of control, trying to find something to
lick. Suddenly Curly, my cocker spaniel,

rushes towards us from the kitchen, barking like crazy.

'Curly! Be quiet!' my Dad's voice booms from my parents' bedroom at the back of the house.

'I've got him, Dad,' I call. 'Go back to sleep.' Dad's not really into pets, so I'm pretty sure *stray* pets aren't going to be his favourite thing either.

I grab Curly by the collar and try to hold him back from the dog, but that just makes him bark even louder and the stray is pushing at the door from the other side. They're too strong for me. They push towards each other until their noses meet. At least then Curly stops barking.

They stand almost frozen with their noses touching. The scruffy dog is much bigger than Curly but it seems more timid and afraid. I open the door a little wider and the big, hairy, brown mess comes in. He and Curly wag their tails and sniff each other all over. They're friends straightaway.

The new dog has no collar. Some people really need a lesson in animal care. I lead Curly into the kitchen and the stray follows along.

I quietly close the kitchen door behind me and assess the situation. I'm going to need my Vet Diary and vet kit to make some observations. I slip off to my room and grab them.

When I come back into the kitchen
the brown dog is wolfing down my dog's
leftover biscuits. Curly's *not* impressed.

I look down at the blank page.

'Well, the first thing you're going to
need is a name,' I say. For some reason,
one pops straight into my head, so
I write it at the top of the page and
begin to make notes.

HECTOR THE DOG

Breed: He is a mixture – a bit like a labrador
crossed with a collie maybe.

Condition: Very skinny with matted hair.
He's smelly and has fleas.

Nature: Hector is a very friendly dog.

I take out my stethoscope and listen to Hector's heartbeat and then I check his eyes and ears. He seems very happy to be touched and examined. Curly keeps pushing his nose into whatever I am doing.

I'll ask Mum to give him a more detailed examination when she wakes up, but the first person I need here is Chelsea, my next-door neighbour and best friend.

Chelsea is nearly a world-famous animal trainer and groomer. She'll be the best person to get Hector ready for his check-up.

I'm worried that if I leave the dogs while I go next door, they'll bark and wake Mum and Dad. I open the fridge to look for something they could eat while I race and get Chelsea.

I push a few things aside until I see the perfect doggy treat – a large bowl of leftover casserole. Hector and Curly look at me and wag their tails happily as I take it from the fridge.

I hunt around for a second dog bowl,

but I can't find one. I spot Max's dinosaur bowl on the sink.

'That'll do,' I say, as I grab it.

I leave the dogs with their feast while I run to the side of the house and call up to Chelsea's open window. It's hard to call out quietly.

'Chelsea! Chelsea!'

I'm just about to call out again when Chelsea's neat, blonde head appears. She's obviously been asleep but there's still not a hair out of place on her head.

'We've got an emergency! Bring your grooming kit and come to my kitchen. And try to be quiet.'

Chelsea nods and disappears inside. I race back to the kitchen.

CHAPTER
2

Being a vet can be messy

I slowly open the kitchen door and then screw up my nose. The smell of the stray dog is really bad. He's eaten all of his casserole and licked his bowl clean. Curly has tipped the dinosaur bowl over and he's licking his way around peas and chunks of carrot and celery on the floor. Hector watches him closely. He looks more than happy to finish up for Curly when he's done.

I step on a pea with my bare foot and it squashes between my toes. I pull a face and hobble to get a tissue just as Chelsea sneaks in.

She covers her nose and mouth with her hand when she sees and then smells Hector.

'Mind the peas,' I say.

'Whoa!' says Chelsea. 'What a mess!'

'I know,' I say. 'We'll clean it up later. But first, we've got to get this dog clean before Dad sees him. Then Mum can check him over.'

'Where did he come from?'

'I found him at our door this morning.'

'He must have known you were nearly a vet, Juliet.'

We both smile.

'Well, he's too big to lift into the laundry tub where we bath Curly,' says Chelsea.

'How about the bath?' I say.

'Really?' says Chelsea. 'Your mum won't mind having a huge, smelly dog in her bathroom?'

'If we're quick and quiet, she won't even know.'

We grab some plastic jugs and sneak the dogs down the hallway to the bathroom. The smell of Hector in the small room is even worse when we close the door. Chelsea holds a handtowel over her nose, but her eyes are still watering.

I turn on the taps to fill the bath.

'Okay Chelsea, help me lift him in,'
I say, after I've got the water to the
right temperature.

It's a struggle, but eventually we
get the big, filthy mess of a dog in the
bath. I turn off the taps and we begin
to pour jugs of warm water over his
back. Thick rivers of brown water run
off his coat.

Chelsea opens her grooming kit and
gets out a small bottle of dog shampoo.
'We might need to use some of your
shampoo as well,' she says.

I grab a bottle from the shelf and
we start to lather Hector all over. He
loves it and stands very still as we rub
and scrub, massage and comb him.

The muck and filth makes the foam a dark-brown colour.

'Why can't you stand still like this when you have a bath, Curly?' I say, turning to look at my cocker spaniel sulking in the corner. He doesn't look too happy about all the attention Hector is getting.

'What are all those little black dots?' asks Chelsea, peering at some froth on her hands.

'Fleas,' I tell her.

Chelsea leaps to her feet and moves away from the bath.

'Fleas?' she squeaks. 'You didn't tell me he had fleas!' She starts checking her arms and legs.

'Of course Hector's got fleas, Chelsea – he's a stray dog. You're going to have to get used to fleas if you want to be a world-famous groomer and trainer.'

Suddenly we hear the toilet flush. We both freeze. There's a tap on the door.

'Juliet, what are you doing?'

It's Mum.

'Um, we have an emergency, Mum,'
I stammer. 'A stray dog came to our
house and . . .'

Just as Mum opens the bathroom
door, Hector decides to shake. The
whole room is suddenly sprayed with

chocolate-coloured, flying, foamy flea-bombs. We all scream. Mum comes in and quickly shuts the door behind her.

'Juliet, what *were* you thinking? Where did it come from? Is that my *good* shampoo?'

'Mum, calm down!' My voice is almost as hysterical as hers. 'We'll clean it all up. He came to our door. We didn't use that much.'

'Is everything all right, Rachel?' Dad is on the other side of the door.

'Yep,' says Mum, glaring at me. 'It will be. Just give us a minute, love.'

'Why would you bath it in here?' Mum whispers through gritted teeth. 'Why didn't you come and get me?

Why didn't you wash it outside?'

I can't keep up with Mum's questions. She's so cross I don't actually think she wants an answer. She takes the jug from me and starts to rinse Hector.

'You girls start wiping down the walls and floor. And put Curly outside.'

When I open the bathroom door to take Curly out, I hear more trouble coming from the kitchen.

'Aw, yuck! What's this all over the floor?' Dad has found the peas, carrot and celery.

'Gross. What's all this brown stuff?' Max has found his dinosaur bowl.

Being a vet can be very complicated.

CHAPTER 3

Being a vet can be tough

'There is no way that dog is staying here!' Dad is not happy about our unexpected visitor.

'I agree,' says Mum. 'I don't think I've seen him at the surgery before, but I'll check and see if we can find his home.' She turns to look at Chelsea and me. 'If we can't, Hector will have to go to the lost dogs' home. If someone's looking for him, that'll be the first place they go.'

Chelsea is still trying to comb the

knots out of Hector's fur. 'If someone did own him, they didn't look after him very well,' she says.

We go with Mum to her surgery and she checks Hector over. He's thin, but other than that, he's healthy enough. Mum lets me scan him for a microchip but he doesn't have one.

'What are microchips anyway?' asks Chelsea.

'They're made from silicon and are about the size of a grain of rice,' I tell her. 'Microchips are injected into an animal's loose skin and each chip has a special code to show who owns it. The codes are read with a scanner like this one.' I pass the scanner to Chelsea, so she can have a turn. 'They're really good if a dog loses its collar.'

Mum double-checks her files, but a dog matching Hector's description has never come into her surgery.

Chelsea and I spend a few hours making Hector look and feel better. We brush him and trim the fur around his eyes and mouth. We even clean his teeth!

Curly has a bath too, in case he picked up some of Hector's fleas. We do it in a large plastic tub that Dad has put outside for us. He's not in the mood for dogs inside after this morning.

Curly stands very still for his bath, which is unusual. He keeps looking over at Hector as Chelsea brushes his coat and quietly talks to him. I think Curly might be just a bit jealous, so I give him a big hug to make him feel special, too.

When both dogs are pampered and beautiful, we tie a lovely blue bow around Hector's neck and take them

for a walk down the street. We stop to talk with every person we meet, but nobody has seen Hector before.

We're both exhausted and very disappointed when we get home.

'Poor Hector,' says Chelsea. 'I don't want to take him to the lost dogs' home. But what can we do?'

'Maybe we could take his photo and make some lost dog posters to put up around the neighbourhood?' I suggest.

We get busy and make a heap of posters. Dad even lets us print them out on his good printer. I think he wants Hector to find his home as much as we do.

We all admire our work as the

HAVE YOU LOST THIS FRIENDLY DOG?

HE WAS FOUND IN DAISY RD ON SATURDAY MORNING. HE IS WELL BEHAVED AND HAPPY TO EAT HIS VEGETABLES WITH HIS DINNER.

PLEASE CALL 99 073 0984 IF YOU KNOW WHERE HE COMES FROM.

printer spits out the copies.

Dad drives us around to put the posters up on posts and walls.

'He can sleep in the garage tonight, but tomorrow we'll have to take him to the lost dogs' home,' says Mum when we get back. 'Sorry, girls, but no one has rung about him.'

I look down and sadly pat Hector's

head as he wags his tail.

'We can't keep him, Juliet. I know it's really hard and very sad, but we can't keep every lost animal that comes in. The lost dogs' home will find him somewhere nice to live.'

I understand that we can't keep him, but when I look at Hector I just want to cry.

He's lying on the floor with his head on Max's lap. Max is showing him his dinosaur collection. I can see Hector loves us already. Why else would he put up with looking at all of Max's dinosaurs?

'We could ask your mum?' I say to Chelsea hopefully.

'I already tried. Twice,' says Chelsea. 'Mum says it wouldn't be fair on Princess and she's probably right.'

I understand why Chelsea's mum said no. Princess is Chelsea's kitten. Her mother was a stray cat we saved once. Princess *really* doesn't like dogs.

Mum lets us give Hector an extra big dinner and we set up a bed for him in the garage. Chelsea's sleeping over tonight and we sit together with him until it's time for bed. He cries a bit when we shut the door but after a while he settles down.

Later that night I'm woken up by another thunderstorm. I can hear

Hector, above all the wind and rain, crying in the garage. I don't know how Chelsea can sleep through all the noise. I put on my dressing gown and Curly and I go and sit with him until the storm passes.

Being a vet can be really sad at times. Someone out there must want a beautiful dog like Hector.

CHAPTER 4

Vets know how to be helpful

The next morning we put Hector in the car and drive to the Mercy Street Home for Lost Dogs. When we get out of the car, the barking from inside the building is crazy. Hector doesn't want to go in and I don't blame him.

Chelsea and I need Mum's help to get him to walk to the entrance and he strains against his leash.

'He hates it here already, Mum.' I can feel myself getting upset again.

'Let's just go in and see what they

think,' says Mum gently.

There's no one at the front counter but there's a bell. Mum rings it and we stand and wait. Chelsea sits with Hector, her arms around his neck.

After quite a long time, a man slides the side door open and enters the room. The sound of the dogs barking is even louder until he shuts it again.

'Sorry to keep you waiting,' he says. 'It's been very busy this weekend. Always is after a storm.'

'We're sorry to add to your load,' says Mum, 'but this dog showed up at our house. I don't suppose anyone has reported a large, shaggy, brown dog missing?'

The man looks at Hector and runs
his finger down his list as he wipes his
forehead with the back of his arm. I look
more closely at him. He has a very kind
face but he looks really tired.

'Nope,' he says. 'No brown shaggy
dogs on the list. Doesn't mean they
won't call though. It was such a
whopper of a storm last night *and*
the night before that I've got dogs
here from two towns away! Of course,
it had to happen when I'm short on
staff. Two of them are on holidays
until next week.'

'I'm a vet,' says Mum. 'Can I give
you a hand?'

'Are you kidding?' says the man.

'I would love an extra hand. Just having someone help to check over them all and see if they have microchips or any injuries would be so helpful.'

'I'm nearly a vet and Chelsea is nearly a world-famous animal trainer and groomer,' I say. 'Can we help, too?'

The man looks at Mum. She smiles and nods her head. 'They're actually a great help to me around the surgery.'

'Well, that's settled then,' says the man, smiling. 'What good luck to have three experts to help me out!'

Mum calls Dad to tell him we're going to help out for the day. She says Dad was very pleased because

he thought she was ringing to say
Hector was coming back home.

Chelsea and I race out to the car
to get our vet and grooming kits.
We never leave home without them.
Vets and groomers always need to be
prepared for emergencies.

The man tells us his name is Paul
and then he leads us into the area
where the dogs are kept.

There are dogs in cages everywhere.
Big dogs, little dogs, long dogs, short
dogs, white dogs, black dogs, spotty
dogs and patchy dogs. I had no idea so
many dogs could get lost.

'It's not normally this bad,' says
Paul, yelling over the barking. 'And

twelve people have already rung to say they're coming for their dogs. Can you believe that before the storm, I only had four dogs here?' Paul opens the last cage on the left where there is a chubby cream-coloured labrador.

We lead Hector inside and they both wag their tails and sniff each other's noses. Maybe he won't mind being here after all? I think. But then Hector turns around and looks back at us through the wire of the cage. He starts to cry.

'It's okay, Hector,' I say, patting him through the wire. He must feel really confused.

Paul sees that I am starting to get upset. 'Hector will be fine,' he says.

'He'll settle down soon.'

'Let's help Paul get these other dogs sorted out and then we can work out where Hector belongs,' says Mum, giving me a hug.

Being a vet can be very emotional.

Paul nods. 'I need to check them all for microchips so we can let the other dog pounds and refuges know what dogs we have here. Then we'll put the dogs that have been claimed into the cages up near the office and bath the ones that are really dirty. Plus they're all going to need food, water, fresh bedding and a walk.'

I whip out my Vet Diary and make some notes.

LOST DOG JOBS:

- Sort out which dogs have been claimed and which ones are still lost.
- Give dirty dogs a bath.
- Feed them.
- Fill up water bowls.
- Get clean bedding for each dog.
- Take dogs for a walk.

'Okay,' says Mum, looking around at the dozens of barking, howling, wagging dogs. 'Let's get to work. Where shall we start?'

Paul races to the office and comes back with his list. 'Girls, if I put a peg on the gate of a cage, it means that dog's owner has been found and they are friendly enough for you to handle.

Here are some leashes. If you could walk them to the empty cages up near the office and check they have food, water and bedding, they'll be fine to wait there for their owners to collect them.'

'Rachel, if you would give me a hand to check all of the unclaimed dogs for injuries and microchips, that would be great.'

'If only Hector had a microchip,' sighs Chelsea.

'Or a collar,' I say.

We both look through the cage at Hector. He stands and wags his tail at us hopefully. I wonder if anyone has ever loved him at all.

CHAPTER
5

Being a vet can be a dirty job

Chelsea and I start moving the dogs with pegs on their cages. We can't help giving them a quick cuddle as we move each of them into their new pens.

'You're going home,' says Chelsea, hugging a fluffy little white dog that wriggles in her arms. 'Yes, you are! Yes, you are!'

A big black labrador with a fancy blue collar with a silver tag that says 'Gus' is next. It takes both of us ages to get Gus to go into his pen and then

he's halfway out again before we can
shut the gate. I'm about to call out
to Paul to help us but then I see he
and Mum are busy with a big spotty
Dalmatian in the far pen.

'I've got an idea,' says Chelsea, and
she runs to the feed area and grabs a
bowl of pellets. 'Maybe this will tempt
him.'

'No wonder you're nearly a world-
famous animal trainer and groomer,'
I laugh, as Gus obediently follows
Chelsea into his pen and starts to wolf
down his food.

A sausage dog is next, then a
poodle, then a dog that looks like
a mix of ten breeds.

At last all of the claimed dogs have been moved. We bring bowls of food and water and a soft blanket for each one. Some of the little dogs don't want to eat but Paul says not to worry because their owners will be here soon.

Next Chelsea and I turn our attention to the six dogs that need bathing. Paul has a very large bathing area that has a showerhead on a hose and a big tub.

'This beats our bathroom,' I whisper to Chelsea and we both laugh.

Chelsea and I decide that I'll bring her the dogs after I've given them a quick check-up and then she'll bath them. After their bath I'll dry them off and give them food and water and clean bedding.

Our first dog is an Australian terrier. He's a solid little thing with stringy brown and black fur that's covered in mud and burrs. Apart from this he seems fine, so I bring him in for a bath. Chelsea is wearing white and I grimace as I hand her the muddy, wet dog.

In no time at all Chelsea has him looking super clean and passes him back to me wrapped in a towel. She really does have a talent for washing dogs. I pass her the next dog and take the terrier back for drying and feeding. Our system works very well and in no time at all we have four very clean dogs.

Next up is a dog that looks like a border collie crossed with something else. It's sitting very quietly in the corner. When I clip on the lead he pulls against it.

'It's all right,' I say, patting him gently. 'We won't hurt you.'

I notice he's shaking and holding up his paw. When I take a closer look I can

see he's caught his dew claw on something and it's bleeding and hanging off.

I grab my Vet Diary and turn back to the page on dew claws to remind myself of what needs to be done. (Mum told me about them once.)

DEW CLAWS:

- Dew claws on a dog are kind of like a thumb, or a big toe on a human.
- They are about 5cm up on the side of a dog's paw.
- Sometimes they're removed because they can catch on things and this can be very painful for the poor dog.

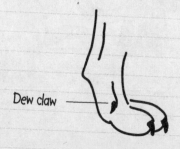

Dew claw

When I find Mum she is running
the microchip scanner over a big dog
while Paul holds the dog steady.

'Mum, one of the dogs has ripped its
dew claw and it's bleeding pretty badly.
I think it might need surgery.'

'Oh, okay,' says Mum. 'I'll come right
away.'

Paul looks at me and nods. I can
see he is impressed that I know what
a dew claw is, but then again every
vet would.

'You're right, Juliet. This little guy
needs surgery to fix that claw,' says
Mum, gently stroking the dog. 'He'll
have to come back with me so it's done

properly. We'll need to bandage his paw up for now. My emergency kit's in the boot of the car, but I know I'm short of bandages. I meant to get some more yesterday.'

'Don't worry, Mum,' I say. 'I've got heaps.' I snap open my vet kit and hold up three bandages of different sizes.

'I'm so lucky you're nearly a vet,' says Mum, smiling. 'But that also explains where all my bandages have gone!'

We watch while Mum bandages the dog's paw and then she takes it to a pen to have a rest until it's time to go.

I look over at Chelsea who has

found an apron from somewhere and still looks incredibly clean and tidy. I haven't washed a dog all day and my clothes are covered in dog hair and spots of mud. How does she do it?

'This is the last one,' I say, passing her a little black ball of fluff with sad eyes. He is shaking all over and obviously doesn't like baths.

'Come on now,' says Chelsea. 'It's nice and warm and we won't hurt you.'

'I might have to hold him,' I say, as the dog leaps around in the tub. When he's wet he looks like a drowned rat and he's really hard to hold still. At one stage he tries to leap out of the bath and knocks the hose out of

Chelsea's hands. Water sprays straight
into my face.

'Oops!' says Chelsea. 'Sorry!'

Both the dog and I are sopping wet,
but we're also a lot cleaner.

I look back down at our list to see
what's next. There are a lot of jobs I can
tick off.

LOST DOG JOBS:

- Sort out which dogs have been claimed and which ones are still lost. ✓
- Give dirty dogs a bath. ✓
- Feed them. ✓
- Fill up water bowls. ✓
- Get clean bedding for each dog.
- Take dogs for a walk.

CHAPTER
6

Vets have lots of good ideas

'Time to take them for a walk,' says
Chelsea.

'It'll be good for them to dry off,'
I say. 'And me!'

We go and see how Mum and Paul
are going.

Everything looks more orderly now.

'Thank goodness for microchips,'
says Paul. 'Nineteen out of the twenty-
eight dogs have homes we can find.
I have all the microchip numbers so
I'll get their details online and start

contacting the owners.'

The dogs have stopped barking and Paul looks much more relaxed than he did this morning. 'You guys have done an amazing job. I could never have done it on my own. Thank you so much,' he says.

'I'll pop back to my surgery with the dog that needs the dew claw removed. It can stay there overnight,' says Mum.

'Is it okay if we take the lost dogs for a short walk to dry them off?' I ask. 'You never know, someone might recognise one of them.'

'It's fine by me,' says Paul. 'That would be a great help.'

'How about you just walk them to

the end of this street and back?' says
Mum. 'And don't take too many at
once. I'll come back for you in about
two hours.'

Chelsea and I choose two dogs each for
the first trip. I choose the fat labrador
and Hector, and Chelsea chooses the
little terrier and the black fluffy dog.

Before we leave, Chelsea puts a
few finishing touches on them. Each
dog is brushed and styled and given
a different-coloured bow to wear
around its neck. No wonder Chelsea's
nearly world-famous, those dogs look
fantastic.

We head off down the street with

our flash-looking pooches. It's quite tricky keeping them all together because they all want to sniff and wee on everything. Luckily we don't have to walk far until we come to a bowls club.

There are heaps of people there. They can't help but stop to admire the dogs. Hector's very happy to meet them all. He wags his tail and circles around them. He gets the most pats because he just loves people. The labrador just wants to sniff their pockets for food.

'Oh, I do miss having a little dog,' says one old lady, bending down to scoop up Chelsea's little black ball of fur. 'We're not allowed to have dogs in the retirement home where I live.'

'They're all lost. We have to try to find their homes,' says Chelsea.

'And if they don't have homes, we need to find them new ones,' I add.

'They seem like nice dogs. It's a pity they're lost,' says an old man. 'Do you

girls work at the lost dogs' home?'

'No, we're just helping out today. We're on school holidays, but we have to go back to school in a week.' I let out a sigh.

We eventually get the dogs past the bowls club and walk them up to the corner and back. There are more people

waiting to say hello to us on the return trip. The dogs love the attention and it seems the older people love giving it. They're all laughing and patting the dogs and telling stories about the pets they once owned.

They're even more excited when we say we'll be bringing another lot.

When we get back to Paul there are three cars parked outside the lost dogs' home and lots of happy people at the front desk. They must have been very worried. I can't imagine what it would be like to lose Curly.

We don't want to disturb Paul when he's so busy, so we swap the dogs over and start to groom the next four.

This time I have the large spotty Dalmatian and a smaller shaggy dog and Chelsea has a sausage dog and a poodle. We head out through the front office again. The lost dogs look very smart with their bows.

'I've never seen dogs from a pound look so lovely,' says one lady to her friend as they watch us walk by.

'I must tell my sister to come and look here. She's looking for a new dog after her poor old Snooky died.'

'Chelsea,' I say, 'that lady has just given me an idea.'

'What?'

'Well, lots of people forget that you can get lovely dogs from pet shelters.

Dogs that are just as nice as dogs from other places, and a lot cheaper, too.'

'You're right,' says Chelsea.

'Well, maybe we need to make more posters like the one we made for Hector? We could put them in pet supply shops and in Mum's surgery. They might even put them in the paper!'

'Juliet, that's brilliant. No wonder you're nearly a vet.'

'Let's start making posters when we get home tonight. Mum has a camera on her phone so we can take some snaps of them before we leave.'

We're so excited talking about our new idea that we're back at the bowls club before we know it. The manager of the bowls club has carried some chairs out to the footpath and there is now a row of smiling faces and warm hands waiting to say hello to us.

We tell them about our idea for the posters and a lady with a long grey plait suggests putting posters in the bowls club too.

When we finally get back to Paul we're exhausted, and Mum drives in just us we unclip the last of the dogs.

'Great news,' says Paul. 'The Australian terrier has been picked up as well, so that leaves us with just eight homeless pooches. Hopefully more of those will go in the next couple of days.'

I smile, even though I was hoping it was Hector that had found his home.

Maybe more posters will help him.

'Paul, can we make some posters about the dogs that need to find a home? We thought it might help.'

'That's a great idea,' says Paul. 'I can copy them and put them on our website, too.'

'Can we come back tomorrow?' I beg Mum. 'Chelsea and I are really going to need to get to know the dogs if we're going to make meaningful posters about them.'

'And they will definitely need more walking and grooming,' adds Chelsea.

'Sure,' say Mum, rolling her eyes just a little. 'As long as it's okay with you, Paul? I have to bring the other dog back anyway.'

'Of course it is!' says Paul. 'How often do I have assistants who are nearly vets and groomers to help me out?'

Chelsea and I can't get the smiles off our faces. We're going to be very busy.

CHAPTER 7

Vets stay up late sometimes

Before we leave the Mercy Street Home for Lost Dogs we get Mum to take some photos of the dogs that need to find a family.

As soon as we get home, we race to Mum's surgery to check on the dog with the sore paw. He's still a bit sleepy from his operation, but Mum says he's going to be fine.

Curly is not too happy when he sniffs our clothes. He can smell other dogs all over us and seems a bit confused.

After we've had a shower and dinner, we load the photos onto the computer and start to make our posters.

'If we put the dog's photo at the top, we can make a checklist to fill out when we observe them tomorrow,' I suggest.

'Great idea,' agrees Chelsea. 'That way people get a quick snapshot of what each dog is like.'

We start to make our checklist.

Name:
Age: Puppy / adult / mature
Sex: Male / Female
Eating habits: eats anything / fussy eater
Likes:

- ☐ Exercise
- ☐ Baths
- ☐ Chasing balls
- ☐ Sleeping
- ☐ Children
- ☐ Chewing things
- ☐ Barking
- ☐ Older people
- ☐ Vegetables

'Time for bed, girls,' says Mum.

Chelsea is sleeping over at my house – I love school holidays.

'Nearly finished, Mum,' I say. 'Can we just have a couple more minutes?'

'Five minutes, then into bed.'

Curly is snuggled up on the floor beside us. I give him a big cuddle.

He's very happy being the top dog again. I hope Hector's not too sad.

'At the bottom we should say to contact the Mercy Street Home for Lost Dogs and include the phone number,' I say.

'Good idea,' says Chelsea, and she types it in.

We fall into bed exhausted. For once, we are both too tired to talk.

Curly wakes me the next morning by licking my toes.

'Yuck, Curly!' I laugh.

We have breakfast and then go out to Mum's surgery to check on the collie with the sore paw.

Mum lets us take him out for a bit of a walk in the garden before we put him in the car to go back to the lost dogs' home.

'I wonder if anyone else has rung about their dog?' says Chelsea on our way there.

I know Chelsea is thinking about Hector as much as I am. Best friends know these things.

When we get there we can tell lots of dogs have gone home because it's heaps quieter.

'We're down to just six now,' Paul reports happily. 'One of the other shelters called looking for the little poodle and the small shaggy dog.'

'Can we go and see Hector?'

'Sure,' says Paul, and he stays to talk to Mum about the collie with the sore foot.

Hector is curled up on a blanket when we go in. A lot of the other dogs jump up and run to the front of their pens, but he doesn't move.

'Hector,' I whisper quietly as we open his door.

Hector leaps up when he hears my voice. He jumps all over both of us and turns around in happy circles. Chelsea and I hug him as hard as we can.

'Come on, Hector,' says Chelsea. 'Let's see what you lost dogs can do.'

CHAPTER
8

Animal trainers are really clever

Paul helps us take the six dogs out into the large yard behind the shed to start our observations.

We tie the dogs to the fence in a line and I sit with a clipboard while Chelsea ties a number on a piece of card around each dog's neck. Paul obviously hasn't seen a trainer as good as Chelsea before, so he sits down to watch.

'Let's start with the food tests,' says Chelsea.

She opens her training kit and

takes out some parcels of different food she has brought from home.

'Um, Chelsea, will your mum mind that you've brought roast lamb, sausages *and* half her vegetables?'

'That's one of the best things about having four huge, football-playing brothers, Juliet. If food disappears, I'm the last person anyone would suspect.'

I nod and look over at Paul. He shrugs his shoulders and frowns a little, but I'm sure he understands that animal trainers must put their animals first.

'Paul, do you have any dry and canned dog food we could use, please?' asks Chelsea.

'Sure. We've got heaps in the shed.'
Paul walks off and soon comes back
with some dog food.

'Okay, let's start with the dry food,'
says Chelsea as she puts a few biscuits
in each dog's bowl. 'When I put them
down, Juliet, could you make a note of
what dog eats what food?'

'Okay,' I say, pencil ready.

She puts the bowls on the ground in
front of each dog. I watch carefully as
the dogs approach their bowls. Some
of them are straight into the dry food,
while others sniff and look away.

Chelsea holds up the next sample
of food and does the same. She keeps
going until the dogs have tried all of

the different foods.

Hector and the labrador love being tested. They're tied up on either side of the little sausage dog. As soon as they finish their food, they strain on their leads to reach his. The sausage dog looks very worried – maybe he thinks he'll be mistaken for a meal!

I draw up a table in my Vet Diary.

Dog number	Breed	Dry food	Canned food	Vegies	Cooked sausage	Roast lamb
1	Dalmation	√	√		√	√
2	Black fluffy dog					√
3	Hector (Mixed breed)	√	√	√	√	√
4	Sausage dog				√	√
5	Labrador	√	√	√	√	√
6	Border collie		√		√	

'From this test we can see who's
fussy and who isn't,' says Chelsea.
'It'll be really helpful when people
enquire about the dogs, Paul. It would
be terrible for someone to choose a dog
they don't fully understand.'

Paul nods. He has a slightly dazed
expression on his face. He's obviously

never seen a world-famous animal
trainer in action before.

'Now let's test some of their other
skills and interests,' says Chelsea.

The phone rings and Paul has to
leave as Chelsea takes some balls and
toys from her bag. She unclips all of the
dogs and throws the tennis ball

down to the other end of the enclosure.

The collie and the Dalmatian take off after it. The sausage dog runs the other way. The black fluffy dog just stares at the other dogs, and the fat labrador sits down and yawns. Hector spends his whole time trying to get as many pats from us as he can.

I take lots of notes as Chelsea continues. She hands the dogs a variety of chew toys that can have food hidden inside them. Only the Dalmatian and Hector show any interest, but Hector has no idea how to get the food from inside the toy. He drops it on the ground in front of him and starts to whimper. The collie is still jumping around waiting for the ball to be thrown again. And the labrador is stretched out and sleeping in the sun.

'Well, this tells me quite a lot,' says Chelsea as she looks down at my notes. 'We can fill in their posters with a lot more detail now. I think the little dogs might suit older people and perhaps the labrador, too. I also think poor Hector has never been given much attention.'

OBSERVATIONS

- The border collie and the Dalmatian can fetch.
- The labrador likes to sleep.
- The Dalmatian and Hector like to chew things.
- The smaller dogs are not very interested in toys or games.
- Hector loves people!

Chelsea is interrupted when Paul calls out to us from the office, 'Girls, the owner of the sausage dog and the black fluffy dog just called. It's an old lady whose friend saw you walking them past the bowls club.'

'Chelsea, you're amazing. You said those little dogs might belong to an older person!' I say, scooping up the sausage dog and giving it a hug. 'Fancy them coming from the same home.'

We update the remaining dogs' posters and then make some copies.

'Let's take them for another walk and put some posters up,' I say. 'Somebody's got to want these lovely dogs!'

CHAPTER 9

Every dog deserves a good home

'You know, Chelsea,' I say quietly, as we walk down the road, 'the dog I'm most worried about is Hector.' I have to whisper because I don't want him to hear me. 'He doesn't really have any talents, except that he loves people.'

'I know,' says Chelsea sadly. 'I really wish we could keep him.'

We get to the bowls club and see a few familiar faces. There doesn't seem to be as many people here today, but a couple of people come out to say hello and pat the dogs.

'Oh, I'm so pleased,' says a little old lady when we tell her some of the dogs have found their homes. 'Every dog deserves a good home.'

Suddenly Hector pricks up his ears and starts to bark.

'Hector, stop it,' I say. He's being a bit naughty now and pulling on his lead. 'Sit!' He just looks at me and coughs from all his pulling. Poor Hector hasn't even been taught how to sit.

The manager comes over to say hello and he offers to put some posters inside the bowls club. He's about to tell us something else when Hector starts pulling and barking again.

'Hector, stop it,' I say. Chelsea leans over to help me hold the lead. He's really going crazy now, jumping around and barking and carrying on.

'Hector, stop it!' I say firmly. I'm embarrassed because he's not making a good impression at all. People expect vets to be good at controlling animals.

Hector won't listen. He is pulling so hard we're being dragged down the path. The other dogs are pulling against us in the opposite direction. Hector is scaring them and creating a huge fuss. People have stopped bowling and are looking over at us.

'Hector! Cut it out!' I yell. Hector spins around so his head is pointing towards us and he's pulling backwards.

'His collar!' Chelsea gasps, just as he pulls it straight over his head and tears off down the street.

'HECCTTTOOOORRRR!' we bellow in unison as the barking dog runs through the carpark and disappears around the back of the bowls club. We can still hear him barking like crazy.

'Please, hold these!' I beg as we pass the leashes of the other three dogs to the people standing with us. I start to panic. I can't bear the thought of Hector getting lost all over again. Being a vet can be terrifying.

We run in the direction of the

barking. The manager follows us.
Maybe he's worried Hector's going to
attack someone.

'I think he's stopped running,'
Chelsea says as we race through the
parked cars.

We turn the corner to see Hector
standing next to something, barking
and wagging his tail. It's an old man.
He's fallen over on the stairs.

'Hector,' says Chelsea. 'Is this what
you were trying to tell us?'

The manager quickly helps the man
up into a sitting position. 'Are you
okay, Bernie?' he asks.

'I'm all right,' says Bernie. 'I'm just
a silly old fool for misjudging those

stairs. I've twisted my ankle.' He leans over and gives Hector a big pat then says, 'I thought I'd be lying here for ages until someone heard me, but this fellow found me straightaway!'

Hector wags his tail happily.

'Well, I'll be darned,' says the manager. 'What a clever dog! You know,

girls, when we were on the footpath
I was just about to tell you the bowls
club has decided to adopt a dog. Lots of
these people live in retirement homes
where they're not allowed to keep pets,
so we thought it'd be nice if there was
a dog here. I was going to choose the
Dalmatian, but I've just changed my
mind. I live at the house attached to
the side there, so at night he could
stay with me.'

'Oh, Hector! Did you hear that?'
Chelsea and I are hugging him all
over. 'Did you hear, Hector? You have a
home. You'll never run out of pats here.
And you'll be close by so we can visit!'

Some more people come and help

Bernie to his feet and we all walk back around to the front of the club.

The manager tells us he'll come to sign Hector's papers and pick him up this afternoon.

We can't wait to tell Paul the good news and we run with the dogs all the way back to the lost dogs' home.

As we walk in I hear Paul telling a family that the dogs at this shelter have all been assessed for their behaviour and food choices. He's showing them our posters about each dog.

I have a feeling it won't be long before the other dogs find homes too!

Right now, it feels *so* good to be nearly a vet.

Juliet
nearly a
Vet

Playground Pets

CHAPTER
1

Sometimes vets need to take charge

It's Monday lunchtime and we're
helping out in the science room at
school. Chelsea and I are cleaning
out the guinea pigs' hutch.

Our science teacher, Mrs Kuss, is
on the phone. Primary schools don't
usually have teachers that just teach
science, but our school does, and that's
why I love it. Vets have to be good at
science.

When Mrs Kuss gets off the phone,

we realise something is wrong. She shakes her head and mutters to herself, 'Oh dear me, this is not good at all.'

'What's wrong?' asks Chelsea, my best friend and neighbour.

Mrs Kuss looks stressed and a bit upset. 'My dad has gone into hospital and needs to have an operation. It isn't anything too serious, but my mother's very worried. I have to take two days off to be with them, but there's so much to organise here. I'm never going to be able to get things ready for the teacher taking my place. I need to catch a plane tonight!'

'We can help the new teacher and look after everything for you,' I say.

'We know how the Green Team works,' adds Chelsea, 'and you know the animals will be fine. After all, Juliet is nearly a vet.'

Mrs Kuss smiles, but she still looks nervous. 'Thanks, girls, I just don't know how on earth someone will be able to come in here and teach all the lessons and run the Green Team, feed the animals, do the composting –'

'Mrs Kuss,' I have to interrupt because she's getting even more upset, 'it's going to be okay. Chelsea and I will make a list of everything that needs to be done, and then we can work out who can do them. You just think about the lessons.'

'Oh what would I do without you, girls?' says Mrs Kuss.

Chelsea and I don't answer her. We don't know what she'd do without us either.

'Right,' says Mrs Kuss. 'I guess I have no choice. I'm just going to have to prepare my lessons in the short time I have and hope whoever Mr Bartlett finds to replace me has lots of experience teaching science.'

I whip out my Vet Diary and turn to a new page.

'Let's go through the jobs and work out who will do them, Chelsea. You go and plan your lessons, Mrs Kuss. We'll get the other things sorted out.'

Vets are good at taking charge when they need to.

Chelsea and I start to think of all the things that need to be done every day in the science room and I write them down.

SCIENCE ROOM JOBS:

• Feed and check the lizards, guinea pigs, stick insects, crickets, mealworms, fish, earthworms and bush cockroaches.

• Fill up the water bottles before each class so everyone can water their plants.

• Make sure the vegies are ready to harvest for the Thursday market.

• Compost all the fruit and vegie scraps.

• Collect the earthworm tea for the market.

'We are going to be busy making sure these jobs are done,' whispers Chelsea. 'Do you think we can manage, Juliet?'

'Of course we can! I'm nearly a vet, so I can handle all the animals, and you're nearly a world-famous animal trainer, Chelsea, so I'm sure you'll be able to keep the recycling boys in line with the composting and other stuff.'

Chelsea nods her head, but she looks a little terrified.

Mrs Kuss is looking through drawers. I can hear her talking to herself as she sorts equipment into boxes.

'The most important thing to do is keep Mrs Kuss calm,' I say to Chelsea. 'She's got enough to worry about and we need her to know we can take care of it.'

I start to rule up my Vet Diary into the days that Mrs Kuss will be gone for. 'Let's make up a timetable so we know what to do each day. We can give it to Mrs Kuss to show her nothing will be forgotten while she's gone.'

'Great idea,' says Chelsea.

I start to write our schedule down.

TIME	TUESDAY	WEDNESDAY
Before school	• Feed animals. • Clean guinea pigs' cage. • Fill bottles for plant-watering. • Put out compost bins.	• Feed animals. • Fill bottles for plant-watering. • Put out compost bins.
Lunch	• Collect compost bins and empty them.	• Collect earthworm tea • Collect compost bins and empty them

'Right,' I say. 'I think that's all we need to remember. I'm sure we can run this place without too many problems. How hard can it be? Let's go and show Mrs Kuss.'

Chelsea grimaces and shrugs her shoulders. She can get a bit nervous about new things.

CHAPTER
2

Vets need to be very supportive

Chelsea and I are both waiting at the science room the next morning when Mr Bartlett, our school principal, walks the replacement teacher down the path.

'I've never seen a teacher wear heels that high to work,' I whisper to Chelsea.

'Ah, girls,' says Mr Bartlett when they reach us. 'This is Miss Fine. She'll be filling in for Mrs Kuss. Miss Fine, this is Juliet and Chelsea. They're the captains of this year's Green Team. They'll be very helpful if you have any questions about our science room.'

'Hello, girls,' Miss Fine says with a smile.

She is very glamorous and not very scientific looking. For a moment I feel just a little nervous for Miss Fine.

Mr Bartlett unlocks the classroom door and they step inside. I'm just about to follow when Chelsea grabs my hand to hold me back.

'Did you see her gorgeous nails? And her beautiful long hair? I just love her dress!' whispers Chelsea.

Sometimes Chelsea and I have very different ideas about things.

'Chelsea, does she look like the type of person who's going to like this job?

Have you ever seen Mrs Kuss wearing high heels like that? How is she going to garden in those?' I ask.

Chelsea stops and frowns. 'She's not like Mrs Kuss at all, is she? But I really do love her dress.'

I shake my head and we enter the science room.

Miss Fine is sitting on a chair in the corner looking pale and Mr Bartlett is

getting her a drink of water.

'Ah, girls,' he says when he sees us. 'Miss Fine got a bit of a fright when she saw the lizards. What are their names again?'

'Digby and Delilah,' I say proudly, heading for the large tank. 'Delilah's due to have her babies next week.'

'Oh dear, are there going to be more of them?' Miss Fine's voice is shaky.

'You don't need to worry, Miss Fine,' says Chelsea. 'I was scared of them too when we first got them, but they're actually lovely.'

'Would you like to have a hold of one?' I suggest helpfully.

'No!' Miss Fine jumps to her feet,

then looks at Mr Bartlett and speaks calmly. 'Um, not right now, thank you, girls. I'll just look at the lesson plans and get organised first.'

'Right,' says Mr Bartlett. 'These girls will help you settle in. And please don't worry about the animals – Mrs Kuss assures me that Juliet is nearly a vet, so she'll look after them all for you.'

Miss Fine giggles nervously and Mr Bartlett leaves the room.

Miss Fine stays sitting on the chair and peers anxiously around the room. She looks like she doesn't know where to start.

'Mrs Kuss left all the equipment you'll need for your lessons in the boxes against the wall, and the lesson plans are on her desk,' says Chelsea helpfully, leading Miss Fine over to them. 'Juliet and I can do the Green Team jobs.'

Chelsea and I get the keys off the hook for the shed while Miss Fine starts to look through the lesson notes.

'Oh my goodness, what is that?' she cries. Miss Fine is back at the chair in the corner, pointing at the large cage across the room. I was wrong about the shoes. She can actually get quite a bit of speed up in them.

'Oh, you'll love them!' coos Chelsea. 'That's Pudding and Custard, our adorable school guinea pigs.'

Miss Fine says nothing, but she slowly shakes her head.

'Don't you like animals?' I ask, looking over at Chelsea with my best 'I-told-you-so' expression.

'Um, well, it's not that I don't like them,' she explains. 'It's just that I grew up in an apartment block and we didn't have room for pets.'

'There's always room for pets, no matter where you live,' I say, not impressed with her excuse. 'You just need to think of some different kinds of pets.' I whip out my Vet Diary and show her my page on pets for small yards and houses and start to list them off for her.

PETS FOR SMALL HOMES:

- Fish
- Stick insects
- Mealworms
- Crickets
- Hermit crabs
- Budgerigars
- Burrowing cockroaches

'Cockroaches! Who on earth has cockroaches for pets?' Miss Fine fans herself with the class roll.

'Um, we do,' says Chelsea with a grimace. She points to Mort and Teeny's tank against the wall. 'They're our giant burrowing cockroaches. But don't worry, they're nothing like the dirty cockroaches that come into houses.'

I know it sounds mean, but I don't think I like this Miss Fine very much.

I can't help saying, 'Yes, burrowing cockroaches are much bigger, Mort's nearly eight centimetres long.'

But as soon as I've said it, I feel bad. And when Miss Fine starts to get teary, I feel even worse. At first it's just a tear rolling down her cheek, then lots of tears, and then she's sobbing.

Chelsea and I look at each other then take a step closer. Chelsea puts her hand on Miss Fine's shoulder and I pass her the tissue box.

'Oh, I'm sorry for crying, girls. What sort of teacher am I? I only finished university a month ago and this is my first chance to teach for two days straight and here I am crying before

I even start. Mr Bartlett said there might be a chance of getting a job here full-time, but I can't even walk over to the desk without breaking into a cold sweat.'

Chelsea speaks first, 'Miss Fine, when I met Juliet, I didn't know anything about animals and, if I'm honest, I was really scared when I first held Juliet's guinea pigs.'

I look at Chelsea. I didn't know that. I couldn't imagine being scared of a guinea pig, but I've grown up around all kinds of animals, so maybe it's easier for me. I start to feel really bad for not being more understanding.

'Miss Fine, you have to trust us.

There's nothing in this classroom that will hurt you. We can do this, together. Chelsea and I can do everything that's needed with the animals and you can just focus on the teaching. Mr Bartlett will see what a good teacher you are, just you wait and see.'

Chelsea grabs a bag for Miss Fine to throw her tissues in.

Pudding, the guinea pig, starts to squeak loudly when she hears the bag rustle. She's got her little paws up on the edge of the cage to see what's coming her way to eat.

'Oops, sorry,' I say, laughing. 'She always does that when she hears a bag rustle. Pudding thinks it means more food.'

Miss Fine laughs as she dabs at her eyes. 'That's actually very cute.'

CHAPTER 3

Vets can be wrong sometimes

'We'll show you how it all works,' I say
to Miss Fine, trying to cheer her up.

'Before each lesson the water bottles
need filling so that each class can
water their own plants in the garden.
I can do this for you in the mornings,
but you'll need to choose someone from
each class to refill them during the
lesson,' Chelsea explains.

'All the kids know how to do it and
it only takes five minutes,' I add.

'Okay,' says Miss Fine, as she quickly

grabs a notepad and scribbles some notes. Maybe we have more in common than I first thought.

'The boys from the recycling team will be down soon to collect the food-scrap bins,' I explain. 'They can be a bit rowdy but Chelsea has four older brothers so she can handle them, can't you, Chelsea?'

Chelsea grimaces and nods slowly. 'I guess so.'

'I'll take care of the animals and try to keep them out of your way until you get used to them,' I continue. 'Animals are a bit like people – sometimes the first impression you get of them is not at all what they turn out to be.'

'You girls are so lovely to help me like this,' says Miss Fine, smiling.

We get to work with our jobs. Chelsea heads over to get the water bottles and I begin cleaning out the guinea pigs' cage. I open the lid and carefully lift them into the box they wait in while I clean. As I lift Custard out I hold him up for Miss Fine to see from across the room.

'This one's called Custard. He's an Abyssinian guinea pig. That's why his hair stands out all over his body.'

Miss Fine nods shyly and says, 'He's very cute, but they do look the tiniest bit ratty, don't they?'

I think about bringing Custard closer to her, but something tells me Miss Fine's not quite ready.

Once the guinea pigs' hutch is clean and they are given some fresh grass and vegetable scraps, I get a carrot out of the fridge and grate it up for the mealworms and crickets.

Miss Fine is putting the equipment out for a class experiment when she looks over at me and sees the label on the mealworm tank. 'Oh worms! I actually don't mind worms. They're not so likely to crawl on you, are they?'

'Well . . .' I say. 'Let me show you something in my Vet Diary.'

I flip open to the page on mealworms and point to the life cycle diagram as I explain.

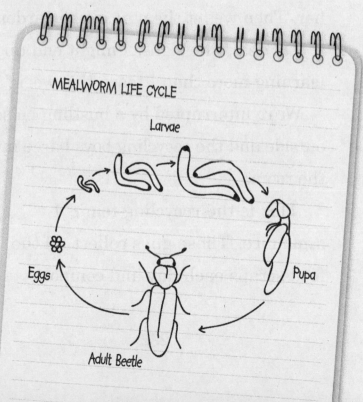

MEALWORM LIFE CYCLE

Larvae

Eggs

Pupa

Adult Beetle

'Mealworms aren't actually worms, Miss Fine, they're the larvae stage of the darkling beetle.'

'And beetles *do* crawl,' says Miss Fine quietly.

'Don't worry, Miss Fine. These mealworms won't turn into beetles for another two months at least,' I reassure her. 'Then we let them go in the garden.'

'Oh dear,' she sighs. 'I might end up learning more than I teach this week.'

We're interrupted by a bustling noise outside and the recycling boys barge into the room.

'This is the recycling team,' I announce. 'These guys collect all the food scraps each day and compost them. They're also really helpful if you ever need any jobs done.'

Josh, Jessie, Mason, Connor, Adam, Liam and Joeshym all stand and look at Miss Fine. For a moment, none of them seem to know what to say.

Then Josh speaks up. 'We also collect snails for the lizards.' He proudly holds up his hand for us to see. It's covered in large, slimy snails.

Miss Fine gasps and steps back. The boys snigger and elbow each other.

'Just make sure you wash your hands with soap after touching them,' I snap.

The boys crowd around the blue-tongue lizard tank and cheer as Digby, the male lizard, demolishes a snail shell in one loud crunch.

Miss Fine flattens her hand against her chest and looks at me in horror. 'They eat live snails?' she asks.

'I know it seems cruel,' I say, 'but we need to try to give the lizards the same food as they eat in the wild. Otherwise they'll get sick.' I turn to my Vet Diary page on blue-tongue lizards and show Miss Fine.

BLUE-TONGUE LIZARDS:

- are reptiles
- belong to the skink family
- are omnivores (eat both meat and plants)
- give birth to live babies
- grow to 60cm long
- and are camouflaged to blend in with leaf litter and hide from predators.

The door opens and Mr Bartlett walks in. 'How are we settling in?' he asks.

Miss Fine's mouth opens but nothing seems to come out.

'Miss Fine and I were just discussing the importance of natural foods for the lizards,' I answer.

'Excellent, keep up the good work,' says Mr Bartlett. 'Let me know if you have any problems.'

'Sure, er . . . of course,' Miss Fine
mumbles as he walks out the door.

'Are you sure you don't want to hold
a snail, Miss Fine?' adds Jessie with a
smirk on his face. I shoot him a glare
that freezes him in his tracks.

The bell goes and it's time to go to
class.

'Chelsea and I will be back at
recess. You'll be okay till then, won't
you?' I ask.

Miss Fine nods, but she doesn't look
very confident. 'None of the animals
can escape?' she asks.

'Nothing will get out,' I say.

Chelsea comes back into the room.

'Bottles are filled,' she says.

'We'll see you in the break,' I say, closing the door behind us.

'Oh dear,' says Chelsea. 'She looks absolutely terrified!'

'She does a bit, doesn't she? We'll have to help her lots this week,' I say, because I really don't want to see Miss Fine cry again.

CHAPTER
4

Vets need to learn damage control

When we come back at recess, I get a feeling there may have been a few problems in the morning classes.

The first thing I notice when I open the door to the science room is Miss Fine's hair. This morning it was all straight and shiny, now she's got it all bunched up with an elastic band. She's limping badly and her hands look like they're covered in blood. And there's water all over the floor around the sinks.

Miss Fine is wobbling her way to the sink when she sees us peering at her from the doorway. 'Well, you probably thought I couldn't do this job, and you were right. Look at this mess and it's only eleven o'clock on my first day!'

Chelsea and I rush to her side.

'Are you hurt?' says Chelsea, full of concern.

'No,' sniffs Miss Fine. 'It would be better if I was though, then I could go home.' She turns on the tap and starts to scrub at her hands.

'What happened?' I ask, looking at a large red stain on the floor.

'I forgot to ask someone to fill the water bottles after the first class,

so when the next group was writing,
I started to do it myself at the sink.'

Miss Fine looks like she might cry
again, but she keeps talking.

'When I looked back at the class,
I saw that a boy had knocked over a
whole bottle of red food colouring and it
was leaking everywhere. I was in such

a rush to clean it up that my heel got caught on the metal strip between the carpet and the lino and broke off.'

She looks at Chelsea and says, 'They were my favourite shoes!'

Chelsea gives a sympathetic nod and pats Miss Fine's back.

'And with all that going on, I forgot

the tap was still on, filling a bottle. There was water everywhere and, of course, that's when Mr Bartlett had to walk past. He opened the door to see how I was going and there I was with bare feet and what looked like blood all over my hands! He was very nice about it, but I could see on his face that he was already thinking of who he could find to replace me.'

Chelsea looks down sadly at the broken shoe as if it is an injured animal and says, 'First we need to find you some shoes.'

Miss Fine doesn't seem to be listening. 'I think I've just learned the first lesson about teaching science. Don't leave kids doing science experiments unsupervised. Ever.'

I make a suggestion. 'What about Mrs Kuss's gumboots? She wears them all the time when she's out in the garden.'

Chelsea looks mortified. 'They'll clash terribly with her dress.' Miss Fine nods in agreement.

I'm rolling my eyes at both of them when the door flies open and Josh and Jessie from the recycling team rush in.

'Whoa!' says Jessie when he sees the red dye and the broken shoe on the floor.

Miss Fine looks at the boys and her lip starts to quiver again.

'Ah, good, you're here,' I say. 'We need some help. Can you go and find Mr C?'

'Mr C is the man that keeps all the things in the school running,' Chelsea explains to Miss Fine.

I pick up the broken shoe and hold it out to Josh. 'Please tell him that we have an emergency, and ask him if there's any way he could fix this shoe.'

'I'd hardly call fixing a shoe an emergency,' sniggers Jessie.

'That just shows how much you don't know. Could you just do it?' snaps Chelsea.

Josh nods quickly and grabs the shoe and they both bolt out the door.

I open the door and yell after them, 'And if you see the other boys, send them over here.'

I turn back to Miss Fine and Chelsea.

'You girls are amazing,' she says. 'Have you ever thought about becoming teachers?'

'Oh, no,' I say. 'I'm going to be a vet and Chelsea's going to be a world-famous animal trainer and groomer.'

'Mind you,' says Chelsea, 'teaching seems a bit like animal training. . . and I'd get to wear nicer shoes.'

We all have a giggle. It's nice to see Miss Fine smiling again.

Chelsea is holding Mrs Kuss's rainbow-patterned gumboots up against Miss Fine's dress to see if they clash when Mason, Connor, Adam, Liam and Joeshym walk in.

'We need your help,' I say to them. The boys nod straightaway because the mess in the room speaks for itself.

'Remember how Mrs Kuss taught us that lemon juice is a weak acid?' I ask them. 'Maybe lemon juice can remove the dye? Mason and Liam, can you get some out of the fridge and start trying to clean it off the floor and table?'

'Sure,' says Mason, and heads for the fridge.

'Joeshym and Connor, can you fill the water bottles for the next lesson, and Adam, can you sweep some of the water away from the door?' I ask.

I'm sure I hear one of them mutter, 'Yes, boss,' but I choose to ignore it.

The boys jump into action. Mrs Kuss always says what a great help they are, and she's right. I guess they can't help it if they're boys.

'Let's check on Delilah,' I say to Chelsea. 'She looked a bit uncomfortable this morning.'

We stand at the tank and take a look at her.

'See how she keeps putting her head up and arching herself back,' I say. 'It looks like she might be going into labour soon to have her babies.'

'Um, do we have to do anything to help with these babies?' says Miss Fine from behind her desk.

'No, she should be okay,' I answer. 'Last year she had seventeen of them without any trouble.'

Miss Fine slumps down onto her chair. 'Seventeen more lizards,' she mutters.

I take out my Vet Diary and start to write some notes on Delilah. Last time she had her babies overnight, so I'm not sure how she was behaving before she went into labour.

298

'My mum's a vet. I'll check with her tonight if that neck-arching thing is normal,' I say.

'I thought lizards laid eggs?' said Miss Fine, still shaking her head and trying to cope with this new information. 'I like eggs. Eggs don't crawl on you.'

'Most lizards lay eggs, but blue-tongues are among a small group that give birth to live young,' I explain.

Mason comes over to the desk and says, 'I think the dye is all out now, Miss Fine.'

'Oh, thank you so much,' she says, smiling. 'That's a relief.'

The bell goes just as the other boys finish up.

Josh and Jessie come rushing into the room, panting. 'We found Mr C and he's going to try to fix the shoe,' Josh explains. 'He said it'll need time to dry though.'

'I guess it's gumboots for me then,' sighs Miss Fine as her next class lines up at the door.

'At least they have rainbow colours on them,' I say.

CHAPTER
5

Vets save lives

We come back at lunchtime and find
the science room is a lot calmer and
Miss Fine seems a lot less frazzled.
Chelsea has a bag of scraps from the
canteen for the guinea pigs. They
squeak like mad when they hear the
bag rustle as we enter the room.

'We're coming, we're coming,' says
Chelsea as Pudding and Custard peer
out from their cage.

I walk straight over to look at Delilah
while Chelsea feeds the guinea pigs.

Delilah is still pushing her head right back and looks very restless.

'She's been doing that all morning,' says Miss Fine as she carries some equipment to the sink.

'It could be normal,' I say hopefully. 'But she does look very uncomfortable.'

The recycling boys have been to collect all the bins and they've carried them around to the composting area.

'So what else needs to be done today?' Miss Fine asks. She looks exhausted.

'That's about it,' says Chelsea. 'We just have to feed the fish and get some fresh leaves for the stick insects and the bush cockroaches. Then spray the insects' tanks with a bit of water to keep the air moist for them. Mondays are our quiet day.'

Miss Fine opens her mouth to say something but only a little whimper comes out. She walks over to the sink to make a cup of coffee.

Chelsea grabs the fish food for the outside fish ponds and I grab some dry gumleaves from the box in the corner for Mort and Teeny.

There is a loud banging on the door.

'We need Mrs Kuss,' says a little boy from Year Two as I open the door.

'Mrs Kuss is away,' I answer.

'There's a baby bird in the drink trough and it's all wet.'

Miss Fine looks at me with wide eyes.

'We'll come and have a look,' I say.

Chelsea, Miss Fine and I are followed by half-a-dozen seven-year-olds as we make our way through the junior school area. There's a large group of children gathered near the drinking trough below the bubblers. The teacher on duty, Mrs Armstrong, is keeping them well back.

She looks over at us sadly as we walk up. 'A baby bird's fallen into the drinking trough. He's sopping wet,' she says, 'and I don't know what to do with him.'

I look down into the trough to find the little damp chick staring up at us and I breathe a sigh of relief.

'It's okay,' I tell everyone. 'This is the best sort of baby bird to find. It's a noisy miner. He's probably been out for his first flying lesson and fallen in.'

'Do we need to find his mother?' asks Mrs Armstrong.

'That's the amazing thing about these birds,' I explain. 'They are communal feeders, so all of the birds in his group take care of him – not just his mum and dad. As soon as we can get him dry enough to squawk, they'll come from everywhere. You can't see them, but they'll be watching us right now. They're really good parents.'

All the children and teachers look around to see if they can spot the adult miner birds in the trees, but there's no sign of them.

I reach in and gently lift the baby bird out, cupping him in my hands. It's a hot day, so he won't take long to dry. I notice Miss Fine take a step back. She really did miss out on the joy of animals when she grew up.

I pat the chick dry with my school shirt and look around for a low branch.

The baby bird puffs himself up in my hands and flutters the water off his little wings.

'Oh, he's adorable,' whispers Chelsea.

'Mrs Armstrong, do you think you could reach that branch?' I ask once I spot the low branch I need.

'I think I could, Juliet,' she says, and the whole group makes its way over.

'Watch this,' I say to the growing group of little kids that are now gathered around us.

Mrs Armstrong gently scoops up the baby bird and places him on the branch.

'Now all we need to do is stand back and wait,' I tell the crowd.

The teachers move the kids back

and we all wait and watch. Nothing
happens for about a minute, then, we
hear the sound I'd been hoping for.

'Meep . . . Meep-meep.' Our little
friend starts to call out.

Noisy miner birds come from
everywhere. They're grey with bright
yellow circles around their eyes. Two of

them take it in turns to shove insects into the miserable chick's mouth.

'Ohhh,' we all say at the same time. Everyone is really excited and happy. It is always nice to save a life. That's why I want to be a vet.

'Wow,' Miss Fine says to Mrs Armstrong. 'She really is nearly a vet.'

Chelsea looks over at me and gives me a big smile.

❖

When we get back to the science room the boys are back from composting and they've washed the bins and turned them upside-down to dry. Miss Fine is very impressed. 'This recycling team is pretty amazing,' she says. The boys look very pleased with themselves.

Mr C walks around the corner with Miss Fine's shoes in his hand. He gives us a big smile.

'Emergency over,' he says.

Miss Fine blushes. 'I'm so sorry,' she says. 'It's been a bit of a disaster today and my shoe breaking just topped it all off. The girls said you might be able to fix it.'

'Well that heel won't be coming off for a good long time. I used my favourite Gorilla Grip glue.'

'Thank you so much,' beams Miss Fine, as she and Chelsea admire the newly repaired shoe.

'You can't even see where it broke!' gasps Chelsea as Miss Fine struggles out of the gumboots.

I shake my head and smile at Mr C. 'Give me gumboots any time,' I mutter to him under my breath.

'I could not agree with you more, Juliet,' he says and winks.

CHAPTER
6

Vets know when something's not right

I go back and check on Delilah once more before I go home. Miss Fine is clearing tables of equipment again but she seems much happier.

'She's still arching her back,' I say.

Miss Fine comes over quite close to the tank. I smile – she's getting braver.

'Are you worried about her?' she asks.

'I am a bit,' I answer. 'Delilah isn't actually due to have her babies for another week. Mrs Kuss really loves

these lizards and I want to make sure
they're all okay when she gets back.'

'How long are they pregnant for?'
Miss Fine asks.

'Around one hundred days. Last
year she was almost exactly on time.
Don't worry, Miss Fine. I'm going to
talk to Mum about it. She'll know
what to do. She really is a vet.'

Later that afternoon Mum and I look
up lots of information about blue-tongue
lizards in labour. We even watch one
giving birth on YouTube. Mum already
knows a lot about lizards, but she
says it can't hurt to learn about other
peoples' experiences with them, because

every lizard is different.

'Most people seem to say the labour is pretty quick,' I say. 'But I'm still a bit worried, Mum.'

'Why don't I come in tomorrow morning and have a look at her? Then hopefully you can stop stressing, Juliet,' Mum says.

Before I go to bed that night I ring Chelsea and we talk about Delilah. She's worried about her too, so we decide we'll go to school early tomorrow morning to check on her.

Chelsea's waiting for me at the car in the morning and Mum drives us both to school. Miss Fine is already there

preparing for the day when we arrive
at the science room.

'Oh, doesn't she look beautiful!'
whispers Chelsea, as I peer into the
lizard tank.

'Yes, but she's still very fat,' I answer,
looking at Delilah.

Chelsea gasps and then realises
the confusion. 'Not Delilah, Juliet. I'm
talking about Miss Fine!'

'Oh,' I say. I look over at Miss Fine
talking to Mum. She has a bright floral
dress on with matching yellow shoes.

'Hopefully those shoes are double
reinforced,' I snigger.

Chelsea freezes me with a killer glare.
Shoes are something we may never

agree on, but that's okay, best friends
are allowed to have different opinions.

'Let's have a look at this girl of
yours,' says Mum, gently lifting
Delilah out of the tank.

The door opens and some of the
recycling boys come in, rowdy as usual.

'Sh!' I hiss.

They tiptoe over to the tank. We
all watch as Mum takes Delilah out
and holds her over the table for a
check-up.

'Well,' says Mum finally. 'She is
enormous and her tummy is very tight.
I agree with you Juliet – she seems to be
pretty uncomfortable. Is she still eating?'

I open my Vet Diary to check then

say, 'Yes, she had two snails yesterday afternoon.'

Mum nods. 'If she was in a lot of pain she wouldn't be eating,' she says. 'Let's leave her for today and if there's still no sign of labour by this afternoon, I'd like to take her back to the surgery and do an ultrasound and see what's happening in her tummy.'

'I thought the babies weren't due until next week?' says Miss Fine with a panicked look in her eyes.

'Don't worry,' I say. 'If they come early, we know how to care for them from the last time Delilah had babies.'

Miss Fine does not look relieved.

Digby, the male lizard, starts to try

and climb the side of the tank. His little stumpy legs are paddling on the smooth surface, but getting him nowhere.

'We'll take Digby out for a quick walk in the sun,' whispers Josh. 'That'll cheer him up.'

Miss Fine looks speechless as the boys carry the lizard towards the door.

'Are they allowed to take it outside?' she whispers.

I don't know why we're all whispering, but it seems the right thing to do when someone is being examined. I nod. 'We often take the lizards out for a walk in the garden. They are very slow-moving and often just sit in the sun.'

Mum strokes Delilah lovingly and

places her back in her tank.

'Thanks, Mum,' I say, giving her a
quick hug.

She and Miss Fine have a chat
and laugh about something, and then
Mum leaves.

I look out the window and watch the
boys all standing around Digby in the
garden, stretched out in the sun.

Chelsea stands on a chair so she can change the lizards' water bowl. 'Oh!' she squeaks. 'There's a baby lizard! Look, Juliet, right there!'

I smack myself up against the glass of the tank. She's right, there *is* a baby in there.

'Is it all right?' Miss Fine asks, joining us.

I gently lift up the baby lizard and it pokes its little blue tongue out at me.

Compared to the babies that were born last year, this one's really big. 'He's good,' I say, laughing. 'He's huge! No wonder Delilah's having trouble.'

Miss Fine smiles at the baby lizard then walks to the door and calls out to

the boys, 'Guys, there's a baby lizard in here!' She goes back to her desk.

The boys bustle like mad to get in the door, then slow down when Chelsea says, 'Quiet!'

'That's awesome,' says Mason, peering down at the baby lizard in my hand.

'It's so cute,' coos Liam.

'Are there any more?' asks Adam.

'We can't see any,' I say. 'Can you?'

The boys all crowd around the tank looking for more newborns. I can't help noticing that Delilah is not looking very comfortable, and is still arching her neck right back.

'I think we should give her some privacy,' I say, and pop the baby lizard back into the tank.

'I agree,' says Chelsea. She goes and grabs an old sheet from the cupboard under the sink. 'Why don't we put this over her tank?'

'Great idea. Maybe Digby could go in the old tank for the day. We just need to put some mulch in the bottom and some food and water for him. The other heat lamp still works so we can put that in, too,' I suggest. 'Where is he?' I ask Liam.

'Joeshym's watching him,' he replies.

'No, I'm not. I'm right here,' says Joeshym. 'I thought Adam was?'

'I came in with you guys,' says Adam. 'I thought Jesse was doing it.'

Jesse shakes his head and holds out his hands.

We all look at each other and then we look out the window. There's no one out there on Digby duty!

CHAPTER
7

Vets have disasters too

We all charge out the door to where
Digby was last seen.

'Stop!' I scream. 'He could have buried
himself anywhere and we don't want to
step on him. Only walk on the path.'

Miss Fine has heard me scream
and comes running outside. 'What is it
Juliet?' she asks.

'Um . . . it's no problem, Miss Fine.
It's just that we seemed to have, sort
of, just for a moment, um . . . lost
Digby in the garden.'

'What?' she squawks, madly looking at the ground around her feet.

'It'll be okay,' I say, sounding a lot calmer than I feel. 'He can't have gone too far.'

Other kids are coming into the garden to see what all the fuss is about.

'I think we should rope it off,' says Josh.

'Good idea,' I say. He and Mason race off to get some rope from the shed.

'Boys, can you stop everyone coming into the garden until we can get it roped off?' says Miss Fine.

They nod and head off to block the three entrance points to the garden.

'He won't cross the concrete paths

because he'll want to stay hidden,'
says Chelsea, 'so he's got to be here
somewhere. The problem is, it's a big
garden and he'll bury himself for sure.'

We're on our hands and knees
looking under plants and running our
fingers through the mulch. Miss Fine
is pacing up and down on the concrete
in her yellow high heels.

At first I think we'll find him pretty quickly – he's not a little lizard, he's about 50 centimetres long – but as time goes on and it gets closer to the morning bell, I start to think of other possibilities.

Chelsea is obviously thinking the same way. 'He couldn't have been caught by something, could he?' she whispers to me as we search.

'Surely not,' I answer with a groan. 'It would have to be something huge to eat a lizard the size of Digby. I'm sure he's just buried himself. But where?'

Miss Fine has started to fill the water bottles herself as the Green Team are all busy lizard-hunting.

She keeps looking up at us and biting her bottom lip nervously. I can see she's worrying about telling Mrs Kuss one of her favourite lizards is lost.

'Miss Fine,' I call out, 'can you please pour one bucket of water into the tops of the three earthworm farms behind you, so we can harvest the worm tea in the break?'

Miss Fine nods slowly and purses her lips as she gingerly lifts one edge of the lid to the first worm farm.

The first bell goes and we all have to go to our classes. What a disastrous start to the day!

'I'm going to ask Mr Stirk if I can stay and keep looking,' suggests Adam. 'I'm sure he'll understand it's an emergency.'

A few of the other boys nod. 'We'll ask our teachers, too,' Liam says.

They bolt off to see if they're allowed to keep looking. I know Chelsea and I won't be able to miss class because we have our spelling test and then we have music straight after that. We're never allowed to miss music lessons.

'At least the area is roped off,' says Chelsea. 'And I'm certain he won't choose to cross the path and allow himself to be out in the open. He'd be seen too easily. You know how he always sneaks from one bit of cover to another.'

Chelsea is really very observant

about animal behaviour. No wonder
she is nearly world-famous.

We come back at recess, but despite the
boys spending two hours searching the
garden, there is still no sign of Digby.
The boys are filthy and exhausted
and the garden looks like it has been
attacked by rampaging bandicoots.

I go inside to check on Delilah and
her baby. She's still arching her back
and there are no more babies. This is
not a good sign. Once they start having
their babies, lizards usually have them
fairly quickly. I'm glad Mum's coming
again this afternoon. Being nearly a
vet can be pretty hectic!

Chelsea and the boys are still out looking in the garden.

'Maybe we should do the worm tea,' I say to Miss Fine when I walk back outside. 'It's market day tomorrow and we'll be really busy. Mrs Kuss always likes to have it done the day before.'

We bend down to fill the empty milk cartons with the brown water that runs from the tap at the bottom of the worm farms.

'So what exactly is this stuff?' asks Miss Fine.

'Well, we call it worm tea, but actually it's worm wee,' I tell her honestly.

Miss Fine's hand slips on the tap and worm wee splashes onto the concrete below . . . and all over her bright yellow shoes.

Miss Fine is, once again, lost for words.

Chelsea comes down from the garden just in time to see the look of horror on Miss Fine's face. 'It's okay, Miss Fine, we'll find him, don't worry!'

Miss Fine just whimpers quietly. I get the feeling she was thinking about her shoes, not Digby.

Chelsea turns to me and says, 'Juliet, this just doesn't make sense. Where can he be?'

'What a disaster!' I say. 'We've lost Digby and I think Delilah might be in real trouble!'

'This is all happening because I'm here,' says Miss Fine. 'Mrs Kuss would know what to do for all these things, but I've got no idea.' She slumps down against the rock wall and dabs at her shoes with a tissue.

Mr Bartlett comes around the corner. 'How's it all going, Miss Fine?' he asks.

'That was a great idea filling up the worm tea today, Miss Fine,' I say.

Mr Bartlett looks up at the boys scouring the garden.

'They're looking for weeds so it's tidy when Mrs Kuss comes back,' says Chelsea brightly. 'Miss Fine thought it would be a nice idea.'

'Good on you, Miss Fine, you're fitting

right in,' says Mr Bartlett. 'I think we'll be able to find lots more work for you here.' Then he continues on his way.

'I can't imagine there would ever be many weeds in the garden with a Green Team like yours,' says Miss Fine.

'Weeds – that's it!' yells Chelsea suddenly.

We both look at her in confusion and the boys stop what they're doing.

'Weeds made me think of it,' she says. 'Where do we put the weeds?'

'Well, der,' says Mason, 'in the compost bin.'

'Where it is dark and cosy and WARM!' says Chelsea. 'And just the place a lizard would love!'

We all race up to the compost bin and lift the lid. There is a space at the bottom that lets the soil out when it's broken down.

'Boys, can you lift the whole thing up, please?' asks Chelsea.

Up goes the drum, out fall leaves, weeds, grass clippings, dirt and a big, fat Digby.

'Digby!' we all scream. He just blinks at us and flashes his blue tongue.

Each of us hug him and pass him on.

'Chelsea, no wonder you are nearly a world-famous animal trainer and groomer!' I laugh.

CHAPTER
8

Vets can change the way people think

Chelsea and I run all the way back to the science room at three o'clock after our last class. When we open the door, Mum is already at Delilah's tank. Surprisingly, so is Miss Fine. Mum turns to me as we come in. At first I can't read her expression.

'Is she okay?' I whisper.

'They all are,' smiles Mum. 'All ten of them.'

Chelsea and I race over to see.

Lovely Delilah has babies scattered all around her. Already they are exploring, eating and drinking. They are *sooo* cute, and exact miniatures of their mother.

'You are so clever, Delilah,' I tell her. 'Mrs Kuss is going to be so excited tomorrow!'

'One, two, three, four, five,' counts Chelsea, 'six, seven, eight, nine . . . where is number ten?'

'Here,' says Miss Fine quietly, and she opens her hands to show the tiny baby lizard nestled happily in them.

I look at Miss Fine and I can't get the smile off my face.

She just nods at me. Once again,

she seems to be lost for words.

I think maybe, just maybe, Miss Fine might be starting to love animals like I do.

Are you nearly a vet?

Take the quizzes about the four stories
to find out!

Quiz 1

1. **To find a pipi on the beach, you should:**
   a. Call it loudly
   b. Look behind your ears
   c. Twist your feet in the sand
   d. Use a magnifying glass

2. **A mullet is a type of:**
   a. Fishing rod
   b. Crab
   c. Fish
   d. Shell

3. **Fishing line left behind is very dangerous for:**
   a. Birds and sea life
   b. Skipping
   c. Fishermen
   d. Boats

4. **Nocturnal animals:**
   a. Sleep all night
   b. Sleep during the day
   c. Never sleep
   d. Sleep upside down

5. **Which of these is not a type of dolphin?**
   a. Spinner
   b. Pilot whale
   c. Bottlenose
   d. Jelly belly

6. **A possum is a type of:**
a. Reptile
b. Guinea pig
c. Bird
d. Mammal

7. **What does a sea cucumber do to protect itself from predators?**
a. Hide
b. Shoot out sticky glue
c. Hide in a salad
d. Tie itself in knots

8. **Which bird would be most likely to eat sausages?**
a. A budgie
b. A dove
c. A peacock
d. A kookaburra

9. **Which is the goanna track?**

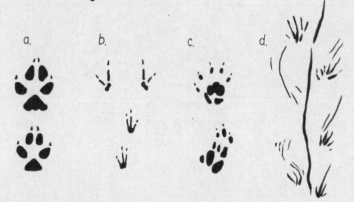

a.　　　b.　　　c.　　　d.

Quiz 2

1. **What did the sun bears eat at the zoo?**
a. Porridge
b. Honey
c. Sunshine
d. Bamboo

2. **What do you need to look in a giraffe's ear?**
a. Binoculars
b. A helicopter
c. A long neck
d. A ladder or platform

3. **Tamarins are a type of:**
a. Turtle
b. Monkey
c. Fruit
d. Meerkat

4. **Why is it dangerous to feed otters?**
a. They have terrible breath
b. They are too big
c. They have sharp teeth
d. They are too slippery

5. **Penguins won't eat fish that are:**
a. Bent
b. Orange
c. Smelly
d. Cute

6. The walnuts are hidden in plastic containers for:

a. Zebras

b. Snakes

c. Capuchin monkeys

d. Sun bears

7. Which of these animals has a shell?

a. Giraffe

b. Elephant

c. Zebra

d. Tortoise

8. Why do some baby animals have to be hand-raised?

a. Their mother dies

b. They get lost

c. Their mother has too many babies

d. Any of the above

9. Which of these baby animal orphans might you have to bottle feed?

a. A baby meerkat

b. A baby blue-tongue lizard

c. A tadpole

d. A baby goldfish

10. Baby elephants can usually stand up:

a. At one day old

b. Almost straight away

c. At three months of age

d. At one year of age

Answers : 1a, 2d, 3b, 4c, 5a, 6c, 7d, 8d, 9a, 10b. Well done!

Quiz 3

1. Dogs often run away in storms because:
a. They love the feeling of rain on their fur
b. They are frightened of thunder
c. They want a better view of the lightning
d. They want to meet up with other runaway dogs

2. Dogs get fleas:
a. To give themselves something to scratch
b. Because they love baths
c. Because the fleas want to suck blood from the dog
d. So they don't feel lonely

3. What should you do if you find a lost dog?
a. Check it for a collar
b. Call the pound to see if someone is missing it
c. Visit a vet to see if it has a microchip
d. All of the above

4. Microchips are:
a. Inserted in the dog's ear
b. Attached to the dog's collar
c. Swallowed by the dog
d. Injected under the dog's skin on its neck

5. Dog shelters:
a. Try to find homes for lost dogs
b. Are often very noisy places
c. Care a lot about dogs
d. All of the above

6. A Dalmatian has:
a. Long curly brown hair
b. Short white hair with black spots
c. Very long, red whiskers
d. Tiny feet and black straight hair

7. Which of these is not a small breed of dog?
a. Labrador
b. Australian terrier
c. Miniature poodle
d. Sausage dog

8. Dew claws are sometimes removed because:
a. They catch on things
b. They don't look good with nail polish
c. Other dogs make fun of them
d. Vets like doing operations for fun

9. How did Juliet meet Hector?
a. Her dad brought him home from work
b. He came to her front door
c. He snuck into Max's bed
d. He booked himself in to the vet surgery

10. Every day, dogs need:
a. Food
b. Water
c. Somewhere warm to sleep
d. All of the above

Answers : 1b, 2c, 3d, 4d, 5d, 6b, 7a, 8a, 9b, 10d. Well done!

Quiz 4

1. Which of these would be a good classroom pet:
a. A bat
b. A monkey
c. A stick insect
d. A sheep

2. What can animals live without?
a. Food
b. Music
c. Water
d. Shelter

3. Mealworms are actually the larvae of:
a. Crickets
b. Bush cockroaches
c. Stick insects
d. Darkling beetles

4. Crickets belong to the group of animals called:
a. Mammals
b. Birds
c. Insects
d. Amphibians

5. Blue-tongue lizards:
a. Lay eggs
b. Feed their young on milk
c. Have moist, slimy skin
d. Give birth to live babies

6. Abyssinian guinea pigs have hair that:
a. Stands up in tufts all over their body
b. Is smooth and straight
c. Only grows on their ears
d. Is normally bright pink

7. A bush cockroach can grow up to:
a. 1 centimetre long
b. 2 centimetres long
c. 8 centimetres long
d. 20 centimetres long

8. Worm 'tea' is good for:
a. Your skin
b. The garden
c. Drinking
d. Your hair

9. Guinea pigs eat:
a. Meat
b. Grass and vegie scraps
c. Absolutely anything
d. Gum leaves

10. To 'recycle' means to
a. Bicycle backwards
b. Buy more new things
c. Re-use something instead of waste it
d. Throw something away

Answers : 1c, 2b, 3d, 4c, 5d, 6a, 7c, 8b, 9b, 10c. Well done!

From Rebecca Johnson

When I was growing up, I was mad about animals.
Not just the normal kind like cats, dogs and
horses, but anything that moved. The best part of
all was that I actually lived next door to a vet!
We are still great friends and he's 95 now. One of
my fondest memories of growing up is going out
in a canoe with my sister and brother after a flood
and rescuing animals that were stranded on sticks
and twigs and ferrying them to safety. Not every
girl I know would be happiest in a canoe full of
mice, bugs and the odd green snake,
but I'm sure Juliet would!

From Kyla May

As a little girl, I always wanted to be a vet. I had
mice, guinea pigs, dogs, goldfish, sea snails, sea
monkeys and tadpoles as pets. I loved looking after
my friend's pets when they went on holidays and
every Saturday I helped out at a pet store.
Now that I'm all grown up, I have the best job in
the world. I get to draw lots of animals for
children's books and for animated TV shows. In my
studio I have two dogs, Jed and Evie, and two cats,
Bosco and Kobe, who love to watch me draw.